THE FINAL

THE FINAL

Jimmy Greaves
and Norman Giller

ARTHUR BARKER LIMITED LONDON
A subsidiary of Weidenfeld (Publishers) Limited

Published in Great Britain by
Arthur Barker Limited
91 Clapham High Street
London SW4 7TA

ISBN 0 213 16723 9

Printed in Great Britain by
Bristol Typesetting Co. Ltd
Barton Manor, St Philips, Bristol

The Beginning of the End

He was waiting for me in the shadows of the players' tunnel as I clattered on my studs down the concrete slope that leads from the Wembley Stadium pitch to the dressing-rooms.

Behind and above me it was sheer bedlam as a hundred thousand voices cheered or jeered the parade of the Anglo-American Cup at the end of a nerve-jarring Final.

I was action-replaying the match in my mind when suddenly he came running up the slope towards me with the urgency of a man chasing a departing bus. My thoughts blurred and reeled like a film coming off its spool. It was all happening in slow motion and it seemed like hours before I realized that he was holding a gun.

'Groves, you bastard!' he shouted as he pointed the gun in the direction of my kneecaps.

Je-sus, I thought, what a way this would be to end my book . . .

1

'YOU know somethin', Eddie? You *look* like a ghost-writer. I've seen more flesh on a dead pigeon.'

Eddie Simms smiled. He was always smiling. It was one reason why I liked having him around. He was easy to be with and had a way of getting information out of you that left you feeling refreshed for having talked to him. Some writers I could name are like muggers the way they come at you in interviews. Crash, bang, wallop. No depth, no style, no nothing. But Eddie was a craftsman. I looked forward to him helping me write my book.

He was thumping away at the push-buttons on his tape-recorder like a hamfisted piano player. 'Shit!' he said, his permanent smile under pressure from just the suggestion of a snarl. 'I can never work these contraptions. The tape's jammed.'

I levered myself out from my armchair, knocking my vodka

and tonic to the floor in the process. 'That's a drink you owe me, Eddie,' I said, crossing the room to my stereo music centre. 'You pour me a large V and T while I fix up my tape-recorder. I'm surprised a leading ghost-writer like you having a cheap Hong Kong job like that.'

Eddie's professional pride was hurt. 'I'll have you know that this "cheap Hong Kong job" as you call it has recorded the voices of some of the world's greatest stars of stage, screen and steam radio,' he said, taking another poke at the push-buttons without getting the tape to budge. 'It gets temperamental only when I'm about to interview bone-headed footballers.'

He smiled and poured me my drink. I liked Eddie.

I uncoiled the microphone wire on my tape-recorder and fed it into the middle of the room, placing the mike on the coffee table between Eddie and my armchair. Just as I dropped myself back into the seat, the telephone rang.

'No peace for the incestuous,' said Eddie as I struggled back up and mimed a kick at the telephone that was on the floor by the cocktail cabinet.

There was a girl on the other end of the line asking if my voice belonged to Jackie Groves.

'This is *the* Jackie Groves,' I said. 'Who is this? Have I had the pleasure?'

There was giggling in my ear. 'Not yet,' she said. 'But I'm ready whenever you are. It's Sally. Remember?'

Sally. Sally? Sally. My mind sent a procession of girls' faces flashing on to my memory screen like a parade of colour slides. Sally came to my rescue.

'You gave me your number last night at Tramp's.'

'Oh, *that* Sally,' I said, trying to recall which of the three girls I'd trusted with my home number was Sally. 'Nice of you to call.'

'I'm ready and available. And willing. What's your address?'

I winked at Eddie who threw a look to the ceiling that told

me he wanted to get on with the interview. She sounded so hot I nearly dropped the telephone.

'Give me two hours, will you, honey? I'm residing at 47 Simpson's Place, Kensington. It's just back of the Royal Albert Hall. Any cabbie will know it. My apartment's on the second floor. No later, no earlier than four o'clock. Okay?'

'You bet, Jackie. It will be a pleasure, I promise. 'Bye.'

I wondered if Eddie noticed the stirring in my trousers as I arranged myself back in the armchair.

'You're not really going to see her at four o'clock?' Eddie asked. He was not smiling. 'Christ, you're playing at 7.30 in a match to decide the championship. And there's the Final on Saturday.'

'Now I know why you're so skinny, Eddie. You worry too much. A little half-hour's amusement is the best possible preparation I could have for the game.' I punished my V and T. 'I don't recall what this Sally looks like but if she's half as good as she sounds wild stallions wouldn't stop me seeing her at four o'clock. And if I gave her my number at Tramp's I must have rated her an "A" class lay.'

Eddie nervously patted at a thicket of fair hair that sat in the middle of his forehead in the old Tony Curtis style. 'D'you think you're being fair to United . . . to your team-mates . . . to the fans . . . to yourself?'

'Shit, Eddie!' I moved uncomfortably in my seat. Lectures were not my scene. 'When did Billy Graham get to you? You know and I know the reason my book is well worth writing is because I am as I am. Do you think you'd be sitting here with me, notebook and tape-recorder at the ready, if I led the sort of choirboy's life the establishment says professional sportsmen should lead? Would Fleet Street be interested in the serialization rights? Think of the headline: "VIRGIN TEETOTAL GROVES REVEALS HOW NOT GOING WITH GIRLS HELPED HIM SCORE GOALS." You might just get the *Catholic Herald* interested in that story. I specifically asked that you should help me with my book, Eddie, because you don't bullshit with words. I'm not interested in producing one of those off-the-top-of-the-head autobiographies that are an insult to the intelligence of the footballer and his ghost-writer. I want us to tell it just as it is. Okay, so I like to screw before a game. That's the way I'm made. It does me no harm and I would like to recommend it as good therapeutic exercise. So it wouldn't suit some other guys. Well, it suits me just fine. Each to his own, Eddie.'

The smile was back on Eddie's face. The ghost-writer had taken command of the evangelist. 'All right, Jackie. You've made your point. Now let's start our first taping session before Sally comes down the alley.'

His smile became a grin. He could be very funny at times. I liked Eddie a lot.

Transcript of Tape-recording No. 1

SIMMS: Let's start at the beginning, Jackie. I know your background pretty well from cuttings. But I don't want this to be a cutting job . . .

GROVES: Right on, baby.

SIMMS: . . . because there are important areas from your youth that are crucial to the overall picture of Jackie Groves. So just talk for a while about your earliest childhood memories.

GROVES: Well as you know, I was born in Duluth, Minnesota. If my dad had gotten his way I would have been born right here in London. But mom wouldn't let dad out of her sight and insisted on going to the States with him when he got his job as a soccer coach in Minnesota. I'm a chip off the old cock. Beg y'pardon, block. My dad used to let his cock rule his head when he was a First Division player back in the late 1940s and through to the late 1950s. We guys like to think we invented screwing but from what some of my dad's old team-mates have told me, he was one of many who played tunes on the old bedsprings before and after matches. Anyways, I was born three months after mom and dad arrived in

Minnesota. You ask about my earliest childhood memories. Well I swear I can recall kicking a football when I was just three years old. My mom always says that the memory is triggered off by the photo that was taken of me at the time. But I can see it in my mind clear as day, kicking the ball to my dad in our back garden while I was wearing one of his England caps.

SIMMS: Which back garden was it? Of the house you were born in?

GROVES: No. Can't remember Minnesota at all. Dad quit his coaching job after less than a year. Wasn't what he'd been promised. You've gotta bear in mind that this was all before soccer took off in the States for real. Americans, the true blue 'uns, used to really mock the game. Fags Football they called it. Only the ethnic groups showed any interest. It helped them cling on to their old-country roots. Dad still had a lot of football left in him but was too proud to go home. Not that there was much incentive. Footballers in England then were earning a maximum £20 a week. Shit, you couldn't keep a family of sparrows on that. So dad went off looking for work and found it down in a place called Fairmount, Indiana. Don't suppose you've heard of the place . . .

SIMMS: It just happens I've been there. I was doing some research on the Wright brothers, Orville and Wilbur. That's where they used to live and where they got their first ideas about flying.

GROVES: Did you interview them?

SIMMS: Very droll. I also learned that the first hamburger and the first ice-cream cone were invented in Fairmount . . .

GROVES: And that James Dean lived and died there, in a car smash. We have just about covered everything that Fairmount is famous for. Anyways, that's where I grew up and where I first started learning how to kick a football. Dad got a job helping out in a restaurant in Fairmount. Finished up owning the place. It was nothing fancy. A posh transport cafe, I suppose you'd call it. But it gave him a fair living.

We lived over the top of the restaurant and my bedroom looked out on to a back garden in which dad erected home-made goals, nets an' all. The neighbours thought he was some sort of fisherman. That's the back garden in which I remember kicking a football at the age of three.

SIMMS : When did you first start playing in organized football?

GROVES : I must have been about seven, maybe eight. Dad had met up with some other Anglos who knew all about his playing days back home in England. They used to spend hours sitting in the restaurant talking about the 'good old days'. I used to sit an' listen and be completely fascinated by stories of the dribbling skills of Stanley Matthews and Tom Finney, the tricks of Clown Prince Len Shackleton, the heading power of Tommy Lawton. All that stuff. I was the only kid in Fairmount third grade who thought of Swift as a goalkeeper and not the author of *Gulliver's Travels.* For every birthday from the age of four my dad used to give me a football. I had my football confiscated at school once and my dad went up and played hell with the Head. I'd been playing with it in the school corridor, running with it at my feet at full speed and imagining I was Stanley Matthews. Finished the run with a shot that smashed the window of a classroom door. The Head, who had played pro American Football in his youth, really bawled me out. He wasn't so much mad that I'd broken the window as that I'd done it with a soccer ball. It was like Carter finding Mao Tse-Tung's little red book on sale in the White House. He bawled me out about playing with a cissy toy in his school and took the ball away. It was the reference to the cissy toy that made dad go bananas. He was in the Head's office first thing the next morning and delivered a lecture on the intricacies of the game of soccer. Must have done a great selling job because the next evening the Head was round at our home looking through dad's cuttings books that mom had kept during his playing career back home in England.

The upshot was that the Head, his name was J. C. – Jesse

– Halas, helped dad and his Anglo pals form a Sunday peanuts soccer league. It was for under-elevens and I was captain and main goal striker of the Fairmount Tigers. We got so that we had fourteen teams in the league, and teams from as far away as Indianapolis joined. Dad was the President of the League and got a real kick out of his involvement. Used to spend hours coaching the kids, me in particular. He always used to say, 'One day, son, you're going to play in front of a hundred thousand crowd at Wembley and score a goal that would have done Dixie Dean proud.' I just wish he'd lived long enough to see Saturday's Final.

SIMMS: We can dedicate the book to your dad.

GROVES: Yeah, that'd be nice. Not that dad would be too proud of some of the stories I'm gonna tell in the book. Make a note for future reference, Eddie, that I must get into the book something that happened to me just last Saturday. I was coming off the pitch at the end of our match at Birmingham when a fan came scrambling over the wall and spat in my face. 'Go home Yank the Wank,' he yelled. I would have broken his neck if I'd got my hands on him but Billy Jones, Birmingham's winger, held me back. The fan, he must have been about thirty-fiveish, was coming back for another spit when two policemen grabbed him and dragged him away. Now that guy, who I'd never seen in my life before, hated my guts. His eyes were blazing hatred. What is it that I've done that makes somebody despise me that much? Why does football bring out so much evil in people? I'd like somewhere inside the book to really analyse how a normal, sane, law-abiding person can be turned into a raving lunatic by the sight of twenty-two players kicking a leather ball around. What have I done to make that man, that stranger, hate me to the point where he invades a pitch to get at me?

SIMMS: It could have had something to do with that winning goal you scored.

GROVES: Come on, Eddie. That's too simple. I expect something better from you.

SIMMS: I agree it's a good subject for analysis but we just haven't got time to go into it today. Just let me briefly say that it's all to do with your lifestyle, your success on the pitch with the football and your success off the pitch with the ladies. You flaunt it all in the face of Joe Public . . .

GROVES: It's not me who flaunts it. It's your crowd. The Fleet Street vultures. I'd be quite happy screwing in private. I've not asked to be projected as if I'm some sort of super stud. Look at what one of the magazines did to me last week. They labelled me 'SOCCER'S CASANOVA, THE STRIKER WHO ALWAYS SCORES BETWEEN THE GOAL POSTS AND THE BED POSTS.'

SIMMS: And you loved every word of it, you sod. Don't give me that crap about it being solely Fleet Street to blame for your image. It wasn't me or any other journalist who posed starkers for the centre spread of *Bedmate*. It was Jackie Groves, *flaunting* it. It wasn't a reporter who nipped off to Majorca in mid-season with Miss Great Britain in tow. It was Jackie Groves *flaunting* it. It wasn't a Fleet Street writer who fell drunk and naked out of a rowing boat on the Serpentine and had to be rescued from drowning by television's busty news-reader, Molly Ashton . . .

GROVES: It was Jackie Groves, *flaunting* it . . .

SIMMS: I could cite dozens of other incidents to help prove my point.

GROVES: It'll make a great book, don't you think?

SIMMS: If we keep getting side-tracked like this, you bugger, the book will never get written. Can we please return to Fairmount and your childhood. What sort of pitches did you used to play on?

GROVES: Our home pitch was a proper football field. Soccer field, that is. My dad talked one of the local farmers into letting us have some grazing land that we marked out. Dad and his friends renovated an old barn and changed it into dressing-rooms, with showers an' all. Used to call our pitch Wembley. It was a good playing surface. The pitch was rolled and cut with loving care. Most other pitches we played on were converted or borrowed baseball pitches which weren't marked properly. Ours was the best pitch in the league and some of the other clubs used to volunteer to play their home fixtures against us on it. Just for the experience of playing at Wembley. Dad was a real ham. At half-time, he'd go and stand in the centre-circle and give exhibitions of ball control. He used to keep the ball up in the air for five minutes, no problem. When they talk about people who helped launch soccer in the States, they should remember the part my dad played. People used to come from miles around down in Indiana just to see what he could do with a football. It got so that the parents of other boys in our team used to go to him for coaching. But most of 'em used to get frustrated and give up quickly. They wanted to do in five minutes what dad had taken a lifetime to learn and perfect.

SIMMS: I was at White Hart Lane once back in the 1950s when I saw your father *juggle* the ball into the net. He kept it bouncing from one thigh to another as he ran past two defenders and the goalkeeper and into the net. You inherited his skill, you lucky sod.

GROVES: Inherited, yes. But I also had to do a helluva lot of grafting to get it right. Dad was a real mean taskmaster. Every morning before going to school and for two hours every evening he had me out in the back garden practising ball control. Trap, flick, half volley. Trap, flick, half volley. I must have put a million shots through those makeshift goals that Dad put up. We used to have one-against-one matches but in our imaginations we were entire teams. Dad would always be Spurs and I'd be England and dad used to say he was Raymond Glendenning and would be the commentator. Have you heard of this guy Glendenning?

SIMMS: Of course. He was radio's voice of football in the 1940s and 1950s. A really popular commentator who could talk at a hundred miles an hour.

GROVES: That's how dad used to do it. 'And Ramsey has

got the ball, passes it to Bailey in midfield who dummies past two men before pushing it through to the feet of Johnny Groves. England goalkeeper Frank Swift' – that was me – 'is advancing from his goal-line but Groves has chipped the ball over his head and into the net. England 13, Spurs 17.' Then when I was on the attack dad would jockey backwards, giving a commentary all the time. 'Finney fires a crossfield pass out to Matthews who sidesteps a challenge from Burgess. Now he's dribbled round the outside of Willis and centres to Lawton who hammers a first-time shot on the volley wide of Ditchburn's despairing dive . . .' God, how dad must have ached for the football he'd left behind in England.

SIMMS: When did he try to get back into the game?

GROVES: It was about 1968. I was ten at the time. Baltimore had a franchise in the North American Soccer League and the general manager wrote dad asking him if he was still involved in soccer and whether they could be of mutual help to each other.

Their idea was that dad could join the Baltimore coaching staff and go to the local schools and colleges where they were trying to get the game accepted at grass roots level. Silly old dad interpreted the letter as meaning Baltimore wanted him to play for them.

He was forty-four years old, for God's sake. He kept on about how Stanley Matthews had played in the English First Division at the age of fifty but blindly lost sight of the fact that he had been out of the game for ten years. Anyway, off he went with his boots and his dreams. He spent a week away up at Baltimore. When he came back he was a changed man. He told my mom that he didn't know whether he or the general manager was the more embarrassed when they both realized there had been a misunderstanding.

They even went so far as to let dad play in a trial match. All his old skills and enthusiasm were there but, of course, his legs had gone. He just couldn't keep up the pace.

Baltimore told him he would be welcome to join the staff

as a coach but that they saw no opening for him as a player. Dad had a look round at Baltimore, decided he preferred Fairmount and came on home with his dreams wrecked.

It was six years later that he died of a heart attack but I reckon he died in the mind and the heart from the moment he realized that he would never again play the game that he loved so much.

SIMMS : Soccer had begun to take off in the States by then. Did you consider starting a playing career out there? I mean, even at sixteen it was obvious you had got your father's skill.

GROVES : It's funny but the thought of playing in the States then just did not appeal to me. After all the talk that had surrounded me for years about football in England my one ambition was to play over here, particularly at Wembley. The *real* Wembley. Anyway, the decision was made easy for me by mom. Once dad died, she couldn't get home quick enough. We were back here in London three months after burying him. I had a trial for United as soon as we settled in with my grandparents in Southgate. United wanted me to join them straight away but mom insisted that I had two years of sixth-form schooling. She didn't want me living only for football like dad.

SIMMS : Just continuing the American theme for a minute, did any clubs show interest in you before you left?

GROVES : I had been approached by a Comets representative after I scored four goals in an Indiana Junior League Cup final. He wanted to take me up to New York to have a look around at their set-up but dad died the following week and that threw all my plans up in the air. I'll tell you this now, Eddie, and it's just between you, me and the tape until things become more positive: I have provisionally agreed to sign for Comets next season . . .

SIMMS : Je-sus . . .

GROVES : It will be a two million dollar deal. I'm sworn to secrecy and I know I can trust you to keep quiet about it. Now that I've got the boyhood bit of playing in the Football

League and representing England out of my system, I want to have a crack at playing in the land of my birth. Like I said earlier, I feel my dad played a part, just a small part, in helping soccer get established in the States and I want to take over the torch. His dream of playing in the States has now become my dream.

SIMMS: I appreciate your faith in trusting me with this secret but for fuck's sake don't blame me if it gets out. I've had enough experience of transfer stories to know that they can never be kept under wraps. When will it be released officially?

GROVES: After Saturday's Anglo-American Cup Final at Wembley. The only people who know, apart from the Comets negotiator, are United manager Scott Ryder, chairman John Turner and secretary Arthur Blake. I signed a provisional contract last night.

SIMMS: I'll bet you any money you like the story is out before Saturday. Ryder, Turner and Blake will no doubt confide in their closest friends who will in turn confide in their closest friends. Somewhere in the chain there will be somebody unscrupulous enough to know they can pick up a lot of money by feeding exclusive information to one of the newspapers.

GROVES: It will be denied all along the line. I can't go into Saturday's Final against the Comets with their players knowing I'm joining them. The player whose place I'm going to take is likely to kick me a hundred miles up in the air!

SIMMS: Bloody hell, what a story. I'd have given my typing fingers for this one when I was a football reporter. Even now the journalist inside me is dying to get to a telephone and dictate the story. It would make a front page splash.

GROVES: Sorry, Eddie. Like me, you've got to live with the secret until after Saturday. Tell you what, I'll let you release it exclusively to one of your Fleet Street contacts after the Final on Saturday. United are going to announce it at a Press conference on Monday morning.

SIMMS: I'll take you up on that but I still wager it will not last until the weekend. No way.

GROVES: We'll see. Now have you any more questions for the book or can I kick you out and get ready to play host to Sally from the alley?

SIMMS: I think this will do for now. What was the name of the school where you did your two years in the sixth form?

GROVES: Clayford Comprehensive. I got seven 'O' levels and an 'A' level certificate in English literature. Also at that school I got my first pass marks in carnal knowledge.

SIMMS: D'you want that in the book?

GROVES: But of course. Let's be honest, it is an important part of my life! I'd only been at the school two months when I was laid – seduced is the way you can put it – by the headmaster's secretary.

SIMMS: You're kidding!

GROVES: No siree. She laid herself out over the Head's desk and invited me in. I kid you not. It was only since I've left the school and talked to other guys who went there that I've found she virtually went through the entire sixth form. She finally ran off with the headmaster.

SIMMS: I'll try to get it in the book but I doubt if the lawyers will pass it.

GROVES: Screw the lawyers. I can call the entire sixth form of Clayford Comp as witnesses.

SIMMS: You mean they watched you at it?

GROVES: No, stupid. But most of them had been there before me. Anyways, she was the first of many hundreds but I'll save those stories for our next taping session.

SIMMS: I think I've got a title for the book.

GROVES: What's that?

SIMMS: *The Soccer Casanova.*

GROVES: Now look who's flaunting it. When is our next taping date?

SIMMS: I wouldn't mind another hour or so after the match tonight. But let's wait and see how you feel when it's over.

I have only until the end of next month to get the manuscript into the hands of the publishers. In view of your pending move to New York it now becomes doubly urgent. I must have a word with the publishers next week about upping the ante.

GROVES: Money. That's all you think of, Mr Thirty Per Cent.

SIMMS: Not true, m'lud. The defendant pleads insolvency. Wait until you've got a wife, four kids and a bank manager to feed.

GROVES: I was only joking, Eddie. You know that. The main reason I let you in on the transfer secret is that I didn't want you having to rewrite great chunks of the book. I take it the first chapter will now be about my return to the United States?

SIMMS: That's for sure. I'll need as many nitty-gritty details about how the transfer was negotiated as possible. We'll talk about it later.

GROVES: How d'you think we'll go tonight?

SIMMS: You mean you and Sally from the alley?

GROVES: Fun-ny.

SIMMS: Put it this way, I just hope Sally doesn't take too much of your energy. Wanderers need a point to take the championship. United must win to become champions. They've got the best defensive record in the First Division and they'll be double-parked on you tonight, that's for sure. I hope United do it but I've got a hunch Wanderers will get the draw they need. With Animal Smith let out of his cage for the evening down the middle of the Wanderers' defence, I don't think he'll be letting anybody past him in one piece.

GROVES: It'll be quite something if we can pull off the League and Anglo-American Cup double in the space of six days. That'll be one for the record books.

SIMMS: Reminds me of 1971. Arsenal beat Spurs on the Monday to pip Leeds for the League championship and on the following Saturday won the FA Cup with an extra-time victory over Liverpool at Wembley.

GROVES: All right, know-all. Now what d'you want me to do with this tape cassette?

SIMMS: I will resist the temptation to give the stock answer. Let me take it with me and I'll return it as soon as I've had it transcribed. Do me a favour, Jackie. If you think of anything that I should know for the book can you note it down or tape it before it goes out of your head?

Transcript of Tape-recording No. 1 Ends

Sally arrived spot on four o'clock. I congratulated myself on my taste. She was a tall, leggy red-head with a Jane Fonda face. I always put a famous face to the girls I lay. It makes remembering easier.

We were both in a hurry. She was flat on her back in my bed within ten minutes of her arrival. It was how I liked it. Uncomplicated. No emotional entanglement. Little dialogue. An out-and-out no-nonsense screw. After twenty minutes of riding high up into the heavens, she was gone from whence she came. Just before leaving, she pecked me lightly on the cheek like a departing aunt and said: 'Thanks.' I never did find out which Sally she was. In my book I'll call her Sally Fonda.

As I dressed to go to the ground for the match, I made up my mind that I owed Eddie Simms and my book an explanation for my obsession with sex.

2

Transcript of Tape-recording No. 2

GROVES: Hi, Eddie. I'm taping this in the car on the way to the ground for the match against Wanderers. I've got nothing better to do. The traffic jam ahead stretches from here to kingdom come. I've been spotted by some fans in a car on my inside. They'll be telling their friends Jackie Groves has gone nuts, 'cos I'm sitting here talking to myself. I just hope you're going to listen to this tape, Eddie, because I've got some things to tell you about my life in the United States that few know about and which have a direct bearing on the way I am. I've never talked before about what I'm gonna tell you now apart from to a shrink in Indiana and I didn't really open up to him. I think it's best that I come out in the open about it in the book, 'cos once I'm transferred to the Comets and am in the headlines in the States somebody down in Fairmount is gonna remember what happened to me and I'd rather *my* version of the story was made public.

It happened when I was nine. It was a real scandal in Fairmount at the time. I recall the *Fairmount News* headlined it 'NINE-YEAR-OLD SEXUALLY ASSAULTED ON THE BANKS OF BACK CREEK'.

As you'll remember from your visit to Fairmount, Back Creek is the thick green stream that runs through the countryside surrounding Fairmount. I was out riding my bicycle alongside the creek one afternoon after school when a farmer from round that way waved me down and asked me if I'd like a drink of lemon. I knew the farmer vaguely. He'd been to see a couple of our games and one of his nephews was in my class at school. Anyways, it was a scorching hot summer's day and I was grateful for the drink that he had in a bottle with him. We sat down on the creek bank and he started to tell me a little bit of history about the place. Y'know, all that baloney about how the town was formed after a troop of soldiers had come down the Mississenewa on the trail of a bunch of Indians and cut the first tracks. Other soldiers travelling east cut a trail for their cannons and where the two paths crossed marked the site of the town. I was fascinated. Always have been in any story that has anything to do with Indians. The next thing I know, this farmer – he was about forty with forearms as wide as tree trunks – was suddenly talking about wrasslin' instead of history. Said he'd been taught to wrassle by the son of an Indian chief. Asked me if I'd like to learn some holds. Well, when you're nine and naive, what do you say? Yes, sirree, please! So we start to wrassle right there on the banks of the Back Creek. I quickly realized that what he meant by wrasslin' was what normal people would call cuddling. I told him I wanted to go home 'cos my dad was expecting me. But his eyes had come wide like a mad dog's and when I cried out in sheer fear he hit me around the head with the butt of his hand. It felt like a hammer hitting me and I passed out.

When I came round, I could feel a pain as if I'd been stabbed in the spine. He was sitting astride me, with his trousers down to his knees. Like the *Fairmount News* later reported, I was being sexually assaulted. I didn't know what was happening to me at the time, only that I was hurting like hell in – how should I phrase it, Eddie? – in my anal area. He was kissing my face and my neck like a big, sloppy dog. I started screaming and kicking, fighting for my life. That man had evil eyes. I could sense that he'd made up his mind to kill me. My life was saved thanks to another farmer who was riding by on his horse when he heard my screams. The man on top of me (I'm deliberately not naming him) jumped off and ran like a scared rabbit. I was taken home and then to hospital where I was treated for bruising and internal bleeding. But most of the damage was to my mind.

By the time I'd recovered my wits to tell the police what had happened, the farmer who'd saved my life by riding by at the right time had rounded up a posse of men including my dad. They'd gone looking for the man who had attacked me and were going to lynch him. But when they got to his farm they found him lying on the verandah with his head shot off. He'd killed himself.

It was three months before I was well enough to go back to school and three years or more before I stopped having nightmares every single night. I still have them now but only rarely, just three or four times a year. What saved me from insanity was my football. I spent every spare second I had with a ball at my feet, using up my energy so that I'd be so plumb tired that I'd fall asleep the moment my head hit the pillow without thinking of that terrifying experience.

I went through hell at school, having to put up with kids sniggering behind my back. They used to point me out as if I was some sort of freak. The nephew of the man who had attacked me put the story around that I was a fag who'd incited his uncle. You know how it is, Eddie. Throw enough shit and some of it's sure to stick. To make matters worse, I read an article in a magazine my dad left lying around that a person sexually assaulted when young often develops homosexual tendencies.

Ever since that headmaster's secretary laid me at school, Jackie Groves has been working overtime at proving that he's no fag. I could call more than three hundred female witnesses to testify that there's nothing lacking in my sexual prowess.

So now you know why I flaunt it, Eddie. I'll give you this tape after the match. For Christ's sake, don't let it get into anybody else's hands. I'm not proud of the story I've just told you but for anybody to understand what makes Jackie Groves tick, then this is the main motivating event in my life. I'm switching off now, Eddie, and will try to put my mind on the match . . .

Transcript of Tape-recording No. 2 Ends

3

TWENTY minutes before the kick-off. Manager Scott Ryder looked like death as he came into the locker-room (I never have been able to get used to calling it dressing-room) to deliver the final team talk. To look at Ryder, you would have thought the last rites would have been more appropriate. His face was haggard and drawn, made old before its time by the nervous pressures of coaxing a team of talented but temperamental footballers to within shooting distance of a remarkable League and Cup double.

Ryder's nerves had just about been shot to pieces and it was common gossip within the club that he was knocking back a bottle of whisky every day. I have to own up and admit that my adventures off the pitch had helped etch many of the deepest lines into his face. A Scottish Presbyterian with a strict moral code, he had tried preaching, pleading and, finally, heavy fines and suspensions to try to make me conform to the rules of behaviour he had set for the United players. I tried, I really tried, to meet his demands but there was a rebel inside me that boiled to the surface every time I began to feel chained by convention. Ryder would release a sigh of relief strong enough to blow me across the Atlantic once the two million dollar deal with the Comets was clinched.

I was more aware than usual of the tension and atmosphere in the locker-room. This was to be my very last League match after five years with United and my mind was taking a series of still photographs of everything and everybody around me for future showing on my memory screen.

Sitting directly opposite me, Irish international goalkeeper Paddy O'Brien was going through his usual superstitious ritual of tossing a ball up fifty-one times and catching it alternately with first his right hand and then his left. It had to be *fifty-one* times. If he ever dropped the ball, he would start again from scratch. Nobody dared interrupt him. We had once deliberately put him off by counting aloud at a faster speed than he was tossing the ball. Paddy let seven goals in that day. We had left him alone with his superstition ever since and it was generally recognized throughout football that he was now the greatest goalkeeper in Europe. When I once asked him the significance of the number fifty-one, he told me with typical Irish logic: 'Well it's one more than fifty.' He was a solemn, introverted character on match days, giving the sort of total concentration to his job that would have given me a headache. But he would drop his mask once the game was over and entertain anybody in listening distance with a non-stop procession of Irish stories.

Alongside Paddy, right-back Ronnie Dicks was tucked over on the bench tying his bootlaces with quick, deft movements of his bony fingers. We nicknamed Ronnie 'The Skeleton' because of a physique that gave him an under-nourished appearance. His looks were misleading. He was one of the fiercest tacklers in the club and had been a British youth boxing champion while at school in Hayes, Middlesex. An intense person with no interests at all outside football, he made up for a lack of basic skills with his determination and commitment to winning the ball. There were several players in the United team who hated my guts. Ronnie Dicks was one of them. A girl he was particularly keen on had made a fool of him at a disco one night by suddenly giving me the sort of kiss you usually reserve for your bed partner. I had given her no encouragement but from that moment on I was no longer welcome in his company, not that it bothered me over much because he bored the arse off me with his incessant talk about football. There were other things in life.

The place next to Dicks was empty apart from an untidy heap of clothes that had been deposited by left-back Roger Hart before he made his usual retreat to the can where he always had a crafty pre-match smoke. Scott Ryder had prohibited smoking anywhere on the ground by players or the coaching staff but had given up on Hart after a long series of stand-up rows and fines. He was a forty-a-day addict and Ryder finally turned a blind eye to his smoking in the lavatory. Hart was a throw-back to the Neanderthal man. He was built like an ape, with forests of black hair covering his chest, arms and shoulders. His conversation was a series of grunts punctuated with the Cockney crutch phrases 'like and that' and 'y'know like' that came at the end of every sentence like full stops. His vocabulary consisted mainly of four-letter words and the only time he could claim an audience was with gutter-level jokes that were an assault on the senses. Hart was totally under the influence of Ronnie Dicks who made the most of finding somebody at last with less intelligence than himself. He had told Hart that I was from a social point of view *persona non grata,* or words to that effect. The only place where Hart could express himself freely and with style was on the soccer pitch. He was one helluva defender who tackled like a clap of thunder and always used the ball with accuracy and vision.

Next along the line was Winner Williams, my closest pal in the club. We had joined United on the same day and went together like scotch and water right from the off. He was a sensitive and erudite Welshman from Pontypool who was nicknamed Winner because in his role as our midfield anchor-man he rarely came out of a tackle without the ball. I was bursting to tell him that I was on my way back to the States, because I knew he ultimately wanted to base himself in America. He had given up studies at Cardiff University to join United and had always regretted not taking his degree. Winner was a devout Welsh Baptist and frowned on my life-style. But he never tried to preach to me and was always first to concede that everybody was entitled to lead their life the way they wanted to. Many of the players at the club were openly envious of the way I dominated the newspaper head-lines for my performances both on and off the pitch but it never used to worry Winner, who hated personal publicity for himself and considered all pressmen parasites not worthy of a moment of his time and concentration. As I looked across at Winner he was taking long and deep breaths, pumping himself up for the match ahead.

He was stocky and powerfully built but appeared small and scrawny alongside Billy Willson, the United captain and centre-half, who stood 6 ft 5 ins in his stockinged feet and had the physique of a weight-lifter. I'd had many drinking sessions with Billy but had been avoiding his company in recent months because he had now become almost alcoholic in his consump-tion and was tending to be more and more violent in the depths of his drunkenness. Right at this moment the club were trying to hush up an incident in which Willson had devastated a bar in the early hours of the morning because the barman had been tactless enough to have questioned the standing of Scotland as a soccer nation. Willson, a man of granite from Aberdeen, 'the granite city', was an established Scottish inter-national and as dominating a central defender as there was anywhere in the world. He didn't know it but he had more reason than most to despise me. I was screwing his wife. But that's another story.

Monty Masters, the supporting central defender, was hunched up on the bench with just his boots, stockings and jockstrap on. Superstition had made him a creature of habit and this was how he arranged himself before every match until just two minutes before our exit from the locker-room. He would then pull his shirt on and finally his shorts before removing his dentures and handing them in a cellophane bag to our trainer, Dusty Rhodes. Masters always insisted on being last on to the pitch and would run along the centre line to the centre spot before joining in the pre-match kick-around. He was a quietly efficient player, making his defensive role look much easier than it was by intelligent positional play that he had perfected in more than fifteen years as a First Division professional. Masters was thirty-four and the veteran of the team. He had joined United at the age of sixteen straight from school in his native Middlesbrough. It had been said of Masters that if you were to cut his wrists his blood would run as blue as the United shirts. He was United through and through and did not hold me in very high esteem. When I returned from my last mid-season jaunt – I had flown to Madeira for an unscheduled six-day holiday – he told me: 'You're a disgrace to United and a disgrace to football. Why don't you piss off back to America?' Monty, who rarely had two words to say for himself, hated me because he felt I was hurting his beloved United. I respected him for speaking his mind.

Sitting farthest from me on my side of the locker-room and looking haunted with fear was Theo Hall, our nineteen-year-old Jamaican-born winger from Birmingham. He had been dressed and ready for action when I arrived at the ground twenty minutes earlier and to my knowledge had made seven visits to the lavatory. Theo had only broken into the first team two months earlier and this was the biggest and most testing night of his life. He had been overawed by all the established star players around him when he first came into the side but had gradually grown in stature and confidence as he realized that he had more than enough skill and speed to hold his own in the First Division. I don't think I'd heard him utter more than a couple of sentences since he had been in the squad but he smiled a lot and was popular with everybody at the club apart from a few dozen moronic racialists on the United terraces. It appeared as if his new-found confidence had deserted him tonight.

In contrast to the anxiety of Hall, Brazilian Paulo Valloso alongside him looked relaxed almost to the point of being disinterested. He had seen it all and done it all as Brazil's midfield schemer in three World Cup campaigns. The English First Division championship was a meaningless prize to him. But along with the rest of us, he was on a £10,000 bonus to win the title and money is a motivator in all languages. Valloso was sitting with his eyes half closed, seemingly half asleep. But it was a common pose and one he sometimes adopted on the pitch. The English Press had dubbed him the Sleeping Panther because of the way he would suddenly snap out of a relaxed spell and light up the game with a moment of sheer genius. He was thirty-two now and his best years were behind him, but he was still a class above any other midfield player in Britain and was a dream for a striker like myself to play with. His passes were always measured and correctly weighted and arrived just where and when you wanted them. This was his second season in English football and he was idolized by the crowds. He spoke fractured English and whenever he got excited, particularly with opponents who were trying to kick him up in the air, he would berate everybody about him in an explosion of Portuguese. After I had last gone missing, Valloso had welcomed me back with a warm handshake and the sincere advice: 'Don't be so loco, man. Girls will always be there but football, it could end tomorrow. Stop being loco.' He meant well.

Studying himself in the mirror between Valloso and me stood United's centre-forward, Mickey Dixon, the most arrogant, self-centred person I had ever known. We could lose a a match six- or seven-one but provided he had scored that one goal he was happy. He was so vain that he would comb his hair seconds before going out on to the pitch so that he would look just right for the photographers. A Cornishman, United had bought him from Bournemouth two years ago as a striking partner for me after his predecessor in the No. 9 shirt, Trevor Beckett, had broken his spine in an early-morning car smash on the M1 motorway. I was dragged out of the wreckage with just minor cuts and bruises. Trevor had been drunk out of his head at the wheel. He paid a terrible price and was now a cripple in a wheelchair. I received a succession of threatening telephone calls and poison pen letters from people claiming the crash had been my fault, but I had only got into the car to try to talk Trevor out of driving home. The accident was really depressing because Trevor was a great player as well as a good friend. Dixon was not fit to lick his boots but the way he swaggered around you would have thought he was God's gift to football and to women. He hated my guts because I scored more goals and was in greater demand with the girls. Dixon was strong in the penalty area and packed a powerful right foot shot but he lacked finesse and his ball control was loose and clumsy. He claimed that I picked up most of my goals by feeding off the mistakes that he had forced defenders to make. While that was true to some extent there was no way I was going to acknowledge his assistance and I knew that with a more skilful centre-forward alongside me I could have scored a lot more goals. Mickey Dixon would consider it the best news of the year when United announced my transfer to the Comets.

On my left sat my wing partner Leftie Wright. You could have chopped off his right leg and it would have made little difference to his game. He did everything with his left foot. He was an old-style winger, sticking close to the touch-line and dribbling around his full-back before firing the ball into the goalmouth. In the course of the last nine months he must have created a dozen goals for both Dixon and me with his pin-pointed centres.

Leftie was a tough little Scouse with a scarred, worn face that looked as if it had been quarried out of the Liverpool paving stones. The zaniest person I had ever known, he always clowned around during training and sometimes in matches and had to take some of the responsibility for the premature ageing of manager Scott Ryder. His passion was motorbikes and he was the only First Division footballer I knew who would come to matches on a 1000 cc Harley Davidson. The club had once tried to ban him from riding the bike but had climbed down when he demanded a transfer. There was always laughter to be heard when Leftie was around. He had been sent off during a UEFA Cup tie in Munich after snatching the flag from a linesman who had waved him off-side and for throwing it javelin-style into the crowd. In a League match at Leeds earlier this season he had walked off the pitch to an ice cream salesman and collected two choc-ices, one of which he proceeded to eat while offering the other one to the referee who booked him for insolence. I would miss Leftie, his humour and his passes. Sitting morosely at the end of the bench was our substitute Frank MacLaren, a versatile Scottish forward who had lost his regular place in the team when Paulo Valloso joined the club. His only full matches that season had been during my two suspensions, one for twenty-one days after being sent off for thumping an Arsenal defender who had been trying to kick my legs off and the other a fourteen-day club suspension following my trip to Madeira. I had gone off on impulse with actress Sarah Gooch and our mid-season romance – that's what the newspapers called it – made front page news. MacLaren thought he had done enough to keep his place and had a shouting match with Scott Ryder when he was relegated to substitute following my return after suspension. 'The only way to get on in this club is to screw every bird in sight,' he had said. A couple of reporters had overheard the row with Ryder and there was a full report in the newspapers. MacLaren had been fined £200 for his outburst and had not spoken a word to me since. He was another who would not be exactly heartbroken when news of my pending transfer was confirmed. MacLaren would no doubt sum up his feelings with the phrase that he and so many footballers used to express elation: 'I'm over the moon.'

Standing alongside Scott Ryder was United coach Hugh Blackley, a former Scottish international defender who was chiefly responsible for our training and tactics. He resented Scott Ryder getting all the credit for our success and we had nicknamed him Mac the Knife because he was doing his best to stab Ryder in the back and get his job. I was hardly Blackley's favourite person. He was a fitness and football fanatic who detested my lifestyle and knew that I had minus-nil respect for him and this theories. It was my opinion that all coaches should be locked together in Dartmoor where they could theorize each other to death. Blackley had taken it personally when I had paraphrased George Bernard Shaw in a newspaper interview: 'He who can, does. He who can't, coaches.' This was not strictly true about Blackley because he had been an outstanding centre-back but he was too defence-conscious for my liking and valued work rate above the skill factor.

The only other person in the locker-room was trainer Dusty Rhodes, a former United player who had known my father well. He was a self-taught physiotherapist and a genius at healing injuries. A Londoner with a sharp Cockney wit, Dusty was scathing in his criticism of the modern footballer and the game in general. He continually delved into the past for anecdotes to illustrate how the game *should* be played. 'Raich Carter wouldn't have played such an obvious ball,' he would say. 'What's lacking today, mate, is imagination. You're a bunch of bloody robots.' He had a point.

Although he carried the title of trainer, Dusty was little more than an odd-job man except when it came to his work in the treatment room. United had a qualified physio but all the players much preferred to be treated by the old Cockney trainer. Scott Ryder had tried to dismiss Rhodes when he first took over as manager six years earlier but had met fierce resistance from the United players, who strongly believed in the healing powers of Dusty's hands. 'When the old Geezer above made me,' he would often say, 'he put the magic touch in me 'ands and me feet but filled me 'ead with sawdust. I couldn't 'ave 'ad any brains to 'ave spent a lifetime in football.' In actual fact he had the same overpowering passion for soccer as my Dad had always had. The old feller was a born cynic and was continually knocking the game. But if he heard one word of criticism of the game from an outsider he would turn on them with a biting defence of the sport he loved.

It had taken just a few minutes for my mind to store these portraits of the men with whom I had shared so many emotions and experiences over the past five years. As I studied them I realized with momentary regret that if there were a popularity poll in that locker-room the name of Jackie Groves would not rate very high.

Yet for all the hurtful, and in some cases hateful, thoughts and feelings we had for each other off the pitch, there was some strange, intangible bond between us that moulded us together as a team. Anybody watching us play together, celebrating our goals and driving each other on to new peaks of effort and endeavour, would have been convinced we were as close and committed to each other as blood brothers. But once the cheering had stopped, the crowds had departed and the adrenalin had been staunched, we resumed our cold wars and went our separate ways. United was a club of cliques and I was an outsider in all of them. I confided only in Winner Williams, himself a loner who preferred his own company. In these searching moments before one of the most demanding matches of my life, I concluded that I was doing the right thing in leaving United.

'This, lads, is what we've been working towards all season,' said Scott Ryder, his right eye twitching with the nervous strain of the moment. 'The next six days will be the most momentous of your lives and in the history of this great club.'

Ryder had lived in England for thirty-five of his fifty years yet his Scottish accent was as thick and as guttural as if he'd just stepped off the Flying Scotsman. He still called football 'fitba', the pitch was the 'park' and his sentences were peppered with 'ochs' and 'ayes' that could have come out of a Robbie Burns poem. His greatest strength as a manager was that he could motivate players with words. The face that had looked like a death mask when he first came into the locker-room was suddenly alive with enthusiasm as he started the pumping process, inflating us for the battle ahead.

'The first thing I want you all to do is empty your minds of any thoughts you may have about next Saturday's Final against the Comets,' he said, looking particularly hard in my direction. 'It's absolutely vital that you give all your attention, all your concentration and all your effort to tonight's game. The League championship is the prize that matters above all. It is proof of consistency and greatness over an entire season. The title is there for you to win tonight.'

He paused for a second, letting us warm ourselves on the glittering prospect of becoming champions. Then he followed up with the bad news. 'You must prepare yourselves mentally and physically for a war,' he said, now walking slowly across the middle of the locker-room like a general inspecting his front-line troops. 'I'm telling you this now so that none of you lose your heads out there tonight. You can expect a lot of intimidation from the Wanderers. They are in the enviable position of knowing they need only draw to take the championship. I've just been handed their team and eight of their players are defence specialists.'

It may have been my imagination but the twitching of his right eye seemed to increase as he looked down the team sheet in his hand. 'It's obvious that they will be packing their midfield,' he sad. 'They'll leave just Boyson and King in our half as the front two in a four-four-two formation.'

'It's likely that they'll drop Thompson back as a sweeper covering behind Smith and Crawford in the centre of the defence.' This was the first contribution from Hugh Blackley, who had just wrestled his head through his tracksuit top and was now dressed ready to take his place on the touch-line bench.

'More than likely,' agreed Ryder, stopping his walkabout to look directly at Mickey Dixon. 'If Thompson does drop back, Mickey, go with him. They'll be trying to get depth in their defence and we mustn't let them swallow us up.'

He turned his gaze first on the terrified Theo Hall and then along the bench to the intense Leftie Wright, who for once actually seemed to be taking things seriously. 'I want you, Theo, and you, Leftie, to play so wide on those wings that you'll be treading on touch-line chalk for much of the evening,' said Ryder. 'We have got to get width in our attack so that we pull their full-backs wide. It's going to be like Piccadilly in the rush hour in front of their goal and we have got to try to make space by intelligent positioning.'

Ryder clenched his fist in a gesture of aggression that didn't need interpretation for the sleepy-looking Paulo Valloso. 'You have got to give us ninety minutes tonight, Paulo,' he said slowly and with great emphasis on the ninety. 'I don't want you flitting in and out of the game like a butterfly. Make up your mind to be first to the ball every time. That midfield is where the battle will be won or lost. You'll find you will have less space than you've ever been allowed in your life. It will be like Brazil against Argentina out there.'

Paulo gave a grim smile. He was a veteran, some would say survivor, of six Brazil-Argentina battles and knew that nothing could match them for brutality and tension. But Ryder's analogy, though exaggerated, had at least awakened his competitive spirit. He tried hard to look on full alert.

I was next for the Ryder treatment. 'It's a racing certainty that Smith will be marking you, Jackie,' he said, leaving it to me to fathom that the word marking has two meanings. Animal Smith had well earned his nickname. His motto was 'Take no prisoners' and legend had it that after every game his right leg was locked in a cage. I'd played six matches against him and had the bruises to prove it.

'He will be trying to make his physical presence felt very early,' added Ryder which, translated, meant Smith was going to try to kick me up in the air as early as possible. 'Don't let him rile you into losing your temper. You know how hot the referees are on retaliation. Lay deeper than usual for the first fifteen minutes or so. He won't want to leave the centre of the defence to come looking for you but try to draw him out if you can. Then Paulo or Winner could nip into the space that he leaves.'

Blackley spoke up from his position in front of the locker-room door. 'It will be no place for faint hearts out there tonight,' he said, his Scottish blood boiling at the prospect of violence. 'If anybody gives less than a hundred per cent they will be letting themselves, their team-mates and the club down.'

He was addressing his remarks to the entire team but I knew they were aimed at me. Because I didn't rush around the pitch like a maniac for ninety minutes Blackley, along with a lot of other people inside the game, was of the opinion that I was lacking in courage and commitment. I preferred to conserve my energy and stamina for the moments that really mattered. My job was to score goals and I couldn't do that if I was spending most of my time back in midfield or defence running my legs off for negative purposes. As for bravery, I didn't see the point in trying to win purple hearts against hired assassins like Animal Smith. I was ready to lay life and limb on the line if there was a half chance of a goal but refused to charge aimlessly into tackles just to prove my manhood. I knew that when it really mattered I was as brave as the next man. Tonight it really mattered.

Ryder was now standing with his back to me addressing the

defence. 'The big danger to us tonight is the quick breakaway goal,' he said. 'Both Boyson and King can move like greased lightning and have picked up most of their goals this season in counter-attacks that have caught defenders out of position pushing forward.'

The warning buzzer rang. We were due out on the pitch in just two minutes. Ryder automatically looked at his watch. 'God, what's happened to the time?' he pleaded. 'I just want you defenders to use your heads. Obviously we need you to be attack-minded tonight. We know we've got to win.'

'Shit or bust,' said blunt Billy Willson.

'That's a fair summary,' Ryder said with a rare smile. 'But keep on your toes for the long ball pumped over your heads for Boyson and King to chase.'

He lightly punched Paddy O'Brien on the shoulder. 'You could get quite lonely tonight,' he said. 'You'll be our goalkeeper and sweeper rolled into one. I want Billy and Monty to push upfield as much as possible, certainly for all deadball situations. You drop back and cover for them Winner.'

We were now all standing up and doing stretching exercises and stamping our studs on the ground to get the feel of our boots. We glistened with liniment and the early spring of sweat that would become a stream and then a river before the evening was through. To an outsider, we must have looked like a dancing troupe rehearsing an African tribal routine.

Ryder was continuing his team talk, close to panic as the clock began to overtake him. 'Paddy, whatever you do don't kick long clearances up into their half,' he pleaded. 'We are going to be outnumbered in midfield and the likelihood is that you will be giving them possession. I want Ronnie and Roger to come back and pick up short goalkicks and clearances. Then play it along the wings. We've got to stretch them as wide as we can to make room in the middle. They'll be looking for Billy to use his height in the box. Hopefully he can pull one or two defenders out of the middle, then while they're positioning themselves for the high ball to the far post Theo and Leftie can play it to the feet of Mickey or Jackie at the near post.'

Blackley unlocked the door ready for our exit. We were all shaking hands with each other like friends meeting for the first time in years. We did it before every match. It was part of the ritual.

Ryder joined in the ceremony, patting each of us on the back and coughing into his fist to mask his emotion and also to clear his throat for one last Churchillian call to arms. 'One day, lads,' he said, 'you will look back on this match as the most important of your lives. Make it a match worth remembering. Don't let Wanderers dictate the way the game is played. And don't let them make you lose your composure. They'll be trying to needle you. With their tongues as well as their tackles. Don't let them get to you. I'll shoot any man who gets himself sent off. We need eleven players out there tonight and everyone of you giving 101 per cent.'

Billy Willson collected a ball from Dusty Rhodes and stood in front of the door waiting for us to fall untidily into line behind him. Monty Masters handed his dentures to Dusty and then went to the back of the queue, his craggy face set in hard, determined lines. I was glad he was on my side tonight.

As Blackley prepared to open the door to let us out, Willson looked over his shoulder and gave a battle order that would not be found in any coaching manual but which said in a short sentence what Scott Ryder had been trying to say for the last ten minutes. 'Right, lads,' he said. 'Let's get out there and stuff 'em.'

A commissionaire handed me an envelope as I walked third in line along the corridor towards the steps that led down to the pitch. We sounded like an army on the march as our studs scraped on the stone-paved floor along which thousands of footballers had walked to and from the battlefield during the ninety-five years of United history. In the distance, at the end of the sixty-yard corridor, there was a crescendo of booing and jeering drowning the cheers of the visiting supporters as Wanderers ran on to the pitch for the match of *their* lives.

Winner Williams nudged me in the ribs with his elbow and winked as I tore open the envelope and took out a note that was written on scented paper: 'See you tonight. Your place. 11.30. Love. J.'

I looked ahead to the broad back of our captain, Billy Willson, and wondered what he would be doing at 11.30 tonight. I knew where his wife would be.

My place. 11.30.

4

IT took Animal Smith just ninety seconds to make his intentions clear. Paulo Valloso slipped the ball into my path as I raced to the edge of the Wanderers' penalty area. I was just about to square it to Mickey Dixon when Smith swung his right boot and coldly and deliberately attempted to kick me in the shins. My instincts for survival saved me and I jumped just in time so that he connected with the studs of my boots. The impact was enough to send me cart-wheeling on to a pitch softened by a heavy pre-match down-pour.

Smith's face was a mask of hate and menace as he reached out a hand in a pretence at helping me up. 'There's plenty more where that came from, you big wanker.' He spat the words out at me as the referee came running towards us from the half-way line.

'Cut that out, No. 6,' shouted the ref, Jeffrey Marshall,

who was one of the most experienced officials in the League. 'Any more of that and you're off.'

That made me laugh. We called him Marshall Twerp because of his weakness with violent players. He often sent players off if they back-chatted him but rarely took action against the cloggers of the game. Smith started to back off towards the defensive wall that the Wanderers were building in readiness to face our free kick. 'I played the ball, ref,' he shouted in protest, adding for my ears only, 'Next time I'll play your fucking leg.'

Animal was in great nick. I reckon they had been feeding him on raw meat for this match. I placed the ball for the free kick which had been awarded a yard outside the penalty area, though I could have sworn Smith had fouled me inside the box.

Valloso made a dummy run as if he was going to take the kick but stepped over the ball, leaving it to me to take a pot at goal. I struck the ball with the outside of my right foot, curling it around the Wanderers wall. Their goalkeeper Terry North was stranded on the wrong side of goal and could only look on like a spectator as the ball struck the far post and bounced back into play.

I was first to reach the loose ball and chipped it over the head of the advancing North and high into the net. Animal Smith looked as sick as if he had been kicked in the balls. 'There are plenty more where that one came from,' I shouted as Winner Williams and Paulo Valloso led me off on a celebration dance. But our private little party quickly became a wake. A linesman had flagged Theo Hall off-side and the ref gave Wanderers a free kick. Theo looked as if he wanted the earth to swallow him up.

Smith, now twenty yards away, gave me a two-fingered gesture and laughed like a reprieved killer.

Scott Ryder was dead right about Wanderers' tactics. They were playing with nine men back in defence and all of them were going out of their way to needle us with verbal insults.

Leftie Wright, of course, saw the funny side. 'They're going to dig a trench in front of their goal next,' he shouted as he ran past me to take our fifth corner in as many minutes. 'I've never been so popular. I've got two of the bastards following me wherever I go.'

Leftie swung a high, outswinging corner into the packed Wanderers' penalty area and Billy Willson went up like a salmon to head the ball forward with every ounce of his considerable power. The ball hammered against the bar so hard that it rebounded almost to the half-way line to be collected by a surprised and grateful Colin Boyson, one of the fastest sprinters in the League. Everybody in the ground sensed the danger and the crowd howled a warning as Boyson raced into our almost empty half. Only Paddy O'Brien stood between him and the goal. He came to the edge of the penalty area to narrow the angle as much as possible and waved his arms like a great green-breasted bird trying to fly. Boyson elected to try to beat Paddy with a lob and lifted the ball over his head. Paddy put up one of his enormous hands but only managed to help the ball on its way into the net. Twenty minutes gone. A goal down. And we were hitting our heads against a brick wall.

As we lined up for the re-start, Billy Willson clapped his hands together and then clenched both fists as if getting ready for a bare-knuckle fight. 'Come on, lads,' he screamed above the taunting cheers and chants of the Wanderers fans. 'We can still stuff this lot. Heads up. Let's go.'

Winner Williams, the best tactical player in our team, shouted towards the bench where Scott Ryder was looking older and more haggard by the minute. 'Get Theo off, boss. His bottle's gone.'

He had not learned that sort of language at Cardiff University. But he was accurate in his assessment of poor Theo. The occasion had got right on top of him. He had jumped so high to avoid one tackle by Animal Smith that I expected him to finish on the roof of the stand.

Ryder cupped an ear in Winner's direction but could not hear him because of the roar of the crowd as Mickey Dixon passed the ball to me from the kick-off. I played it back to Valloso who pinged a perfect pass to the feet of Hall. He took it smoothly in his stride, sent two Wanderers defenders the wrong way with a clever feint and dribbled daringly past a clumsy challenge from the Animal before firing a low cross shot inches the wrong side of the near post. We all applauded this moment of magic from Theo whose broad grin almost outshone the floodlights as the confidence surged back into him as if he had received a transfusion. I looked back at Winner who shrugged and smiled as I cupped a hand to my ear in a take-off of Scott Ryder.

Wanderers now unashamedly pulled all their players back into their own half, including their two front-line strikers. Leftie Wright needed treatment for a kick in the thigh and as Dusty Rhodes sprayed the bruised and grazed skin with pain-killer he shouted to Mickey Dixon: 'The boss says he wants you to go out on the wings. Try to take their centre 'alf out of the middle.'

Marshall Twerp waved an admonishing finger. 'You're on the pitch to administer first-aid,' he lectured, 'not to give a tactical talk.'

Dusty glared up at the ref. 'The tackles you're letting that bleedin' lot get away with,' he fumed, 'it's a wonder I'm not on 'ere giving a bleedin' leg transplant.'

Marshall, who had been ignoring all sorts of criminal assaults by the Wanderers' defence in general and Animal Smith in particular, snapped a hand to his pocket like a gun-fighter going for the draw. He flicked out a yellow card and held it high over poor old Dusty's head. 'What's your name, trainer?' he demanded. 'You're booked!'

This was too much for Leftie. 'You're a fucking disgrace, ref,' he yelled, pushing off Dusty's attempt to silence him. 'You should stick your whistle up your arse. It would blow better.'

Marshall Twerp was going for his pocket again and you could hear the intake of breath from 55,000 fans as he flashed a red card in Dusty's face. 'Take this player off the pitch, trainer,' he ordered. 'He can take no further part in the game.'

Billy Willson came running from twenty yards away, the sight of the red card acting like a red flag to a mad bull. 'What the fuck's going on?' he roared. 'Surely you're not sending him off. What harm's he doing lying there?'

Dusty had gone as white as one of his spotless towels. The blood had been drained from his face by a mixture of rage and fear over the trouble he had innocently caused. He started to pick Leftie up to put him over his shoulder for the fireman's carry he always uses when taking off an an injured player. 'Get the sub on,' he shouted to Billy. 'I'm taking Leftie off because he's too injured to carry on.'

Now it was Marshall's turn to go white. He started waving his red card around like a magician holding up a playing card for all the audience to see. 'Don't try to be clever with me, trainer,' he said in his best headmasterish voice. 'This player has been sent off.'

Scott Ryder came hurrying on to the pitch. He looked in need of a fireman's carry. 'What the hell's happening here?' he inquired of the referee, his mouth struggling to form the words, he was in such a state of shock.

'I have sent No.11 off for abusive and ungentlemanly behaviour, Mr Ryder,' explained Marshall, almost relieved that he had found somebody to whom he could pass the responsibility. 'I want you to get him off the pitch immediately and your trainer is also banned from taking any further part in the game.'

It was Leftie Wright who was first to accept the ref's ruling. 'Sorry I've let you down, lads,' he shouted. 'But you can beat these morons with eight men. Good luck.'

There were tears of anger and annoyance in his eyes as he limped slowly back to the dressing-room. Dusty handed his trainer's bag to Hugh Blackley and joined Leftie on the long, lonely walk.

Ryder opened his arms wide and looked appealingly to the skies. Then he returned with a shrug of resignation to his touch-line seat and I restarted the game with a free kick for the tackle that had injured Leftie and started all the fuss. I feigned another try at a curler round the wall but instead pushed a short pass into the path of Mickey Dixon who ballooned his shot over the bar.

Animal Smith laughed out loud.

Leftie Wright was sitting huddled in the middle of the bath when we came back into the dressing-room at half-time. Valloso, who had been jabbering away in the direction of the referee in violent Portuguese all the way up the corridor, switched suddenly to his fractured English when he saw Leftie. 'You unlucky man,' he said. 'The referee's loco. The son of an whore. In Brazil he would be hung for this.'

'Don't show him any sympathy.' It was the voice of Scott Ryder who had followed us into the dressing-room, moving quickly but heavily like a mourner late for a funeral. 'I warned you all clearly enough. I told you what it would be like out there. It was the duty of every one of you to stay on the pitch for the full ninety minutes.'

Leftie punched at the water in fury and frustration. 'Sorry boss. I know I've let you down. The ref's a king-size bastard, though. He's letting them get away with murder out there.'

Dusty Rhodes sat in the far corner of the dressing-room, feeling redundant and sick. 'Don't blame Leftie, boss,' he appealed. 'The ref needs shooting.'

This started Valloso off again. 'He's the son of an whore. In Brazil the crowd would have torn his head from his body and kicked it around like a football.'

Before any of us could dwell on the full horror of that scenario, Ryder snapped into his manager-motivator's role. 'Right, forget the first half,' he instructed. 'It was a shambles.

We're playing with our feet but not our heads. We have got to out-think this lot. So far we have played it exactly the way they want us to. We must be more subtle in our approach. We're pumping too many hopeful balls down the middle. Mickey's getting no change down there . . .'

Dixon's pride was hurt. 'I'm outnumbered three to bloody one,' he moaned. 'It's no picnic out there ...'

Ryder ignored the interruption. '... so we've got to try to get round the back of them.'

Winner Williams, sipping tea from a blue mug that had the United crest decorating one side, said: 'I think we should try to catch them out on the left. They're going to be mentally relaxed on that side now that Leftie's out of the game.'

'Exactly,' said Ryer, turning to face left-back Roger Hart. 'I'm counting on you, Rog, to play as if you're Leftie. Don't line up at outside-left at the kick-off but hug that touch-line and get round the back of them at every opportunity.'

Theo Hall's head was down and he was staring miserably at the floor. 'Head up, Theo,' said Ryder, sensing that the youngster needed pumping up. 'That run of yours after they'd scored the goal was the best thing we've seen out there so far. Let's see more of it in the second half. Take them on, lad. Take them on.'

Ryder slipped back into his mourner's mood and coach Hugh Blackley took the opportunity to make his contribution. 'You're all bunching too much in their half,' he said. 'You've got to make space for yourselves. Hold back and let the ball do the work. Be patient. It's no good running around at a hundred miles per hour if you're not getting anywhere. Slow it down and play possession football in midfield. You've got to try and tempt them to come and get the ball.'

He came and stood directly in front of me. 'You're letting Smith swallow you up,' he said. 'All right, so he's showing you his studs and intimidating you. But you've got to expect that. There's a lot at stake out there. For both sides. You're chickening out of tackles and Smithy is loving it.'

I knew Blackley's motives for this spiteful attack. He was trying to get me wound up so that I would take Smith on in man-to-man situations. I didn't need Blackley to light my touchpaper. The Animal had given me all the incentive I needed to try to run him into the ground in the second half.

As we left the dressing-room to resume hostilities, Leftie Wright was still huddled in the middle of the bath. And he was crying like a baby.

The second half was just two minutes old when Roger Hart made a long run down the left touch-line. No defenders picked him up because they were too busy concentrating on pre-planned marking jobs. Sensing danger, Gerry Johnson, who had been double-parked on me along with Animal Smith, suddenly took off in Hart's direction. He slid into a tackle and missed as Hart accelerated past him.

I ran parallel with Hart, the Animal in close attendance. We were just fifteen yards from goal when Hart released a pass that was deflected behind me. I turned and controlled the ball with Smith menacing at my back. Mickey Dixon was screaming for the ball at the far post but there was no way I could get it to him through the forest of legs as the Wanderers defenders gathered like vultures to cut out all scoring options.

Smith was growling threats into my neck and was so close I could feel his breath. 'Try anything clever, wanker, and you're a hospital case,' he said. He had hardly got the words out when I back-heeled the ball between his legs, whipped past him and fired a right foot shot into the top near corner of the net with goalkeeper North and Mickey Dixon waiting at the far post for a pass that never came.

I ran on past the goal in celebration and also to get as far away from the Animal as possible. Roger Hart, whose brilliant run down the left had created the goal chance, leapt on my back like a drunken cowboy. He had well earned his ride. A posse of photographers were back-pedalling in front of us firing off pictures as fast as they could go. 'You should see

Smithy's face,' one yelled from behind his camera. 'He doesn't know you've gone past him yet!'

Billy Willson cut our goal party short. 'Och, the goal of the season,' he boomed. 'Fabulous stuff. But now we've got to do it again. A point is not enough. Come on lads. Let's concentrate on the *next* goal.'

You could hardly hear yourself think for the noise of the United supporters. The goal had driven them potty and they were in full voice. From the North Bank terrace came the chant the supporters had used ever since I had established myself as a player on the pitch and a ram off it:

He's our Yankee Doodle dandy
He's our randy shooting guy
Jack-ie Gro-ves . . . Jack-ie Gro-ves . . .

The Wanderers reacted to the goal by dropping deeper and more aggressively into defence. They were ready to protect their net at all costs and for the next thirty minutes kicked anything that moved. The Animal was firing daggers at me with his eyes but I had not given him an opportunity to get in the crippling tackle that he had promised me. I was deliberately playing deep in the hope that I could lure him out of the middle.

With the game into its last fifteen minutes, the ref reacted to a wild tackle on Theo Hall by calling the two captains together in the middle of the pitch. 'Tell your players to cut out the kicking or I will abandon the match,' he said. 'I am being lenient because of the pressure of the occasion but I will not stand for any more of it. Let's play the last few minutes of the match in a dignified way.'

I looked down the pitch at Animal Smith and wondered whether he even knew the meaning of the word dignity.

Billy Willson spread his arms in a gesture of innocence. 'All we want to do is kick the ball,' he protested. 'It's his lot that are doing the kicking. It's about time you sorted them out, ref.'

Wanderers captain Gerry Johnson, knowing he was just minutes from the championship, told the ref what was obvious to everybody: 'You abandon this match, ref, and you'll have 55,000 fans wanting to lynch you. Let's get on and get the game finished.'

Marshall looked nervously towards the terraces. 'All right, but you've been warned,' he said, his voice lacking his earlier authority and confidence. 'Any more kicking and I shall be getting the red card out.'

Theo Hall had been kicked out of the game and Frank MacLaren came on in his place as we re-started the match with a free kick that produced a well-directed header from Mickey Dixon which North did well to save at full stretch. MacLaren hurried to my side and said: 'The boss says he wants you to move up alongside Mickey. There are only twelve minutes left. I've got to play wide on the right.'

I gave MacLaren a thumbs up sign but with no intention of following the instruction. It would be suicidal for me to move up alongside Dixon. Animal Smith was waiting to kick me to kingdom come and there was less space up there than in a telephone box.

There were only three minutes left now and I was gambling on knowing Smith's moronic mentality. Valloso put the ball to my feet ten yards outside the Wanderers penalty area. Despite screams from my team-mates to 'get rid of it', I deliberately stood with my foot on the ball and stared in Smith's direction. The Animal took the bait and came charging at me like a runaway buffalo. As he approached with murder in mind, I chipped the ball over his head into the space behind him. Winner Williams sprinted after it and struck the sweetest of shots high into the roof of the net from fifteen yards.

The crowd were screaming 'G–O–A–L' as Smith reached me with both feet raised in about the area of my crutch. I instinctively went into reverse gear and backed off sufficiently to avoid lasting damage that would have brought a premature end to my screwing career. I escaped with a grazed thigh and ripped shorts. Even Marshall Twerp was moved into positive action by this attempted assault and battery and held the red card up in front of Smith's face. The Animal spat at my feet and walked off, disgusted and disgraced, in the direction of the dressing-rooms.

We hardly let the Wanderers get a sniff of the ball in the last couple of minutes, playing possession football with lots of first-time passes that had them running in circles trying to recover it.

When the final whistle went, we hugged and danced with each other like consenting adults. A few dozen fans managed to clear the fences around the pitch and joined in our celebrations, helping us to carry big Billy Willson around the ground as if he were the League championship trophy. The Wanderers were pig sick and trudged sadly off the pitch after perfunctory handshakes of congratulation. I could guess how they were feeling. They'd all missed out on £10,000-a-man bonuses.

The League President came on to the pitch and handed the trophy to Willson. We ran a lap of honour and then danced our way to the dressing-rooms. My Football League career was over.

They were action replaying highlights of the match on the television in the Press Interview Room. Billy Willson, Winner Williams, Roger Hart and I had joined Scott Ryder for the after-match Press conference.

Eddie Simms was there and I handed him the tape I had made in the car on the way to the ground. 'Come round the flat in the morning and we can have another taping session,' I told him. 'We've been given tomorrow off.'

'Harry Smith seemed to have a lot to say to you all through the match,' said the *Sun*. 'What was he saying?'

I looked across at Eddie and gave him a smile which, interpreted, meant I was saving that answer for the book. 'He was just discussing the state of the economy and wanted to know where I was going to spend my summer holidays,' I said, earning a strained laugh from reporters who were being driven to distraction by a deadline that waits for no man.

'Did he connect when he made the tackle that got him sent off?' asked the *Mirror*.

I pitched my voice two octaves higher. 'If he had, you would now be interviewing Miss Jackie Groves,' I said, now dropping my voice to normal pitch. 'The only damage was a grazed thigh and a torn pair of shorts. It was worth taking the risk of being gelded to make the space for Winner. He took the scoring chance brilliantly.'

'What did Smith say to you before he went off?' the *Sun* persisted.

'He wished me luck for the remainder of the season,' I replied. The *Sun* man was not amused and so I quickly added: 'What could he say? He knew he had just cost Wanderers the championship. If he had not committed himself to trying to make the tackle we would never have found space in their penalty area. Actually he didn't say anything when the ref sent him off. All he did was to clear his throat. In my direction.'

'Was it instinct or planning when you back-heeled the ball through Smith's legs for the first goal?' asked the *Mail*.

I shrugged my shoulders. 'What can I say, without seeming to have as big a head as some of my critics say I've got? You've seen me nutmeg players before. Obviously there was luck involved but yes, I did know exactly what I was doing when I back-heeled the ball.'

The *Express* man was on the telephone in the far corner of the room, dictating his match report. Suddenly he broke off to shout: 'Don't let Scott Ryder and Jackie Groves leave the room.'

The *Star* reporter looked up from his notebook. 'What's this, then. A hi-Jack?'

We all watched the *Express* man dramatically throw his

telephone down and walk purposefully across the room. 'Your little secret's out, Scott,' he said to Ryder, who was just about returning to the land of the living after the tension and excitement of the last few hours. 'There's a report just come over on the agency tapes from New York that the Comets are going to buy Jackie Groves for two million dollars.'

The years crowded in on Ryder's face again. I looked at Eddie Simms who shrugged and smiled as much as to say: 'What did I tell you?'

5

MY place. 11.30. Jennie Willson was bang on time. And bang is the operative word. I'll say this for the captain's wife. She certainly has her priorities right. We had been screwing for half an hour before she even mentioned New York.

'What's this about the New York Comets then?' she asked, as she lay back on the bed smoking a cigarette while waiting for me to get my second wind. I was not at my best tonight. The game had taken a lot out of me and the graze on my thigh was irritating and smarting.

'What about the New York Comets?' I countered as innocently as possible.

'I heard a news flash on the car radio on my way over here. Something about you joining the Comets for two million dollars. Is this true?'

'For your ears only, yes.' Like Eddie Simms said, a transfer story like this could not be kept secret for long.

'What do you mean for my ears only?' She looked at me as if she was seeing me for the first time. 'I told you. I heard it on the radio on the way here. The whole world knows.'

'Both the Comets and United are going to deny it until after Saturday's Final. We told the Press tonight that there was no foundation to the story. It would put too much pressure on everybody if I were to play against the Comets in the Final with all the players knowing that my next match would be for them.'

She stubbed her cigarette out in the ashtray on the bedside table. As she turned away from me I lightly ran my fingers down her back. I felt my second wind bringing me strength where it mattered. She reached behind her with her right hand and felt me rise. It was time for her to put her priorities right again. Question time was over for now.

I put both arms around her and gently stroked her nipples, feeling them grow firm under my touch. She shuddered and purred like a cat having its fur fondled. Pulling her knees up, she reached back again with her right hand and guided my new-found strength deep inside her from behind. A versatile girl, the captain's wife.

Another cigarette. More questions. This time with an edge that disturbed me.

'How does this leave us then?' she asked, blowing smoke towards the bedroom ceiling. I read danger in the smoke signal.

'How does what leave us?' I knew what was coming.

'You going to New York. How does it leave us? What are we going to do?'

There was, for the want of a more appropriate phrase, a pregnant pause. Then she added: 'About us. You and me.'

I wanted to kick her out of bed and tell her to get back to her husband. But I'm at my least defensive when I'm in bed.

'How do you want it to leave us?' I asked, biting my tongue the moment the words were out.

'We can't just let it end, can we.' She wasn't asking a question. She was making a statement. It sounded as if it had been lifted from a Barbara Cartland novel.

'There will only be the Atlantic between us. The price of a Laker Skytrain.' I was being deliberately flippant. The serious tone in her voice was worrying me stiff. And there's only one sort of stiff that I like to be in bed.

She suddenly sat up as if she had arrived at some momentous decision. She had. 'I'm going to get a divorce from Billy,' she said. 'He's become a hopeless drunkard. I want to come to New York with you.'

I didn't have the strength to sit up. If I had been sitting up I'm sure I would have fallen back into a lying position. I quickly started to establish my defences. 'Look, Jen, I can understand you wanting to get out of Billy's life. He seems set on drinking his way to an early grave. But no way can I see why you would want to come into my life.'

'I'm not thinking about marriage,' she said, as if it were even a germ of a thought in my mind. 'We can live together in New York. They all do it out there. No need for a stupid ring.'

Take Jennie Willson to New York? It would be like taking sand to the Sahara. I decided the time had come for a hard line.

'Sorry, Jen, but it's just not on. We've had a great six months together but remember, right from the start, we made a pact about no emotional involvement. It's been a straight screwing relationship and it's been great.'

Her eyes flashed knives at me as she reached down into the cellars of her mind and came up with memories of her Scottish puritanical upbringing. 'What do you think I am?' she inquired angrily. 'Some sort of whore? Are you trying to say there have been no feelings between us? That it's just been sex for the sake of sex.'

That was exactly what I had been saying. 'I don't want a long-term entanglement with any woman,' I said. 'Not with you, Jennie. Not with anybody. You're a cracking bird. Great in bed and lovely out of bed. You deserve a better deal than you've got with Billy but don't look at me as your liferaft. I will never be able to give myself to any one woman. Never.'

She jumped out of bed as if I'd scolded her and started dressing. Tears were rolling down her face, leaving a dried river of mascara under both eyes.

'It's that Pam Stoughton, isn't it!' she said, as if answering a question that had been asked hours previously. 'You've still got your cock into the vice-chairman's wife.'

That annoyed me. 'I haven't been with Pam Stoughton for six months,' I shot back. 'If you must know, I dropped her off my visiting list when she started talking about divorcing her twat of a husband so that she could marry me.'

There was a glass of vodka and tonic on the bedside table. She picked it up and threw the contents in my face. 'Billy's right what he says about you,' she said through sobs. 'You've got your brains in your balls.'

Charming, I thought. Fucking charming.

My place. 2.30. I was awake in my bed, the sheets still damp from the V and T attack. I was damp with sweat. For the first time in months I had been shocked out of my sleep by the nightmare of what had happened to me as a kid in Fairmount.

It must have been that tape-recording that I did for Eddie. It had stirred up old memories and opened old wounds. In my recurring nightmare I am held in a strangler's grip by the farmer's tree-trunk arms. He is ramming away at my back and when I lift my face to look at him he is headless. That's when I wake up, sometimes screaming with fear and terror.

I couldn't get back to sleep, so I got up, mixed myself a drink, switched on the electric fire and taped some more recollections for Eddie Simms.

Transcript of Tape-recording No. 3

GROVES: Good morning, Eddie. It's 2.40 am Tuesday. I've got nothing better to do so I thought I'd record another tape for the book. I'm feeling real low at the moment. It's the old problem. Women. Why can't they just be satisfied with a bed relationship? Why do they have to go and spoil it by talking about moving in? Marriage even. I envy you, d'you know that Eddie? You've got a stable, settled marriage, four great kids and you know exactly what you want out of life. Me, I couldn't tell you where I'm going if you paid me. Or even where I want to go in life.

When I was a kid I used to dream of one day helping a team win the English League championship. Yet last night's game left me feeling, I don't know ... I guess the word I'm looking for is empty. Yeah, that's it. Empty. I have no sense of achievement. Maybe it's because I'm leaving the club but I didn't feel part of the team in the dressing-room afterwards when all the bubbly was being drunk and the pats on the back were being handed round. I got to thinking what dad would have thought had he been there to see the game. That would have given it all some meaning for me. You have to remember that all my dreams as a kid were fashioned out of his memories of football over here. He'd have been real proud to have seen me score that goal. Particularly as I made Animal Smith look such a banana. Dad hated players like Smith. Players who have a skill only for kicking lumps out of opponents with more talent.

You were at the Press conference and heard them ask what Smith was saying to me during the match. They'd have to have printed their newspapers on asbestos if I'd told them. This brings me to an area I want us to examine regarding the book. If we're going to write it as it really is, we've got to get a lot of swearing into the dialogue. Nearly every other word from Smith last night was either an 'f', a 'c' or a 'w'. I guess it would be called industrial language. The language of the terraces is also the language of the pitch.

Even some of the referees get in on the swearing bit. Strangely enough, the three refs I know who swear a lot on the pitch are among the best we have in the game. It somehow makes them more human when they tell you to get on with the 'effing' game. You feel as if they're from the same world and not from another planet, like some refs seem to be. Marshall Twerp last night, for instance. He was letting Wanderers kick shit out of us. The wonder was none of us got broken limbs. Yet Dusty Rhodes and Leftie Wright get the red card for giving him some lip.

Anyway, here's an anecdote I've remembered for the book. It happened during the England tour last summer. We were stopping at a big, swish hotel in Gothenburg. It was scorching hot when we arrived at the hotel and while the officials were booking us into the rooms we searched around and found it had an indoor swimming pool. Charlie Jenkins, Nobby Clarke and I decided we wanted to swim. There and then. We threw off our clothes and jumped bollock naked into the pool. After we'd been splashing around for about five minutes, I dived to the bottom to see how deep it was. The far side of the pool was made up of a large glass wall and sitting in the restaurant and looking directly at me were about a dozen people. I don't know who was more shocked. I almost drowned from laughing.

It was on that trip that Charlie, Nobby and I proved three into one *does* go. Leave Charlie and Nobby's names out of it but on the night after the Sweden match, which we won four–one incidentally, the three of us were entertained to some incredible acrobatics by a hotel receptionist. She could get her body into some astonishing positions and at one stage . . . correction, at several stages, she managed to accommodate Charlie, Nobby and me inside her at one and the same time. I'll spare a happily married man like you the details but let's just say she was a well-drilled lady.

Another thing about the book, Ed. What references are we going to make to your colleagues? The Press lads. I don't see how we can avoid mentioning some of them. Some of my best drinking and screwing sessions have been in company with TV and newspaper reporters. Particularly abroad. They always have time to make reconnaissance trips to find the best night spots while we're training.

I'll leave you to decide whether we should put names to them but d'you remember that night in Rio after the Brazil match? We all got pissed out of our heads. Our combined team of England internationals and Fleet Street journalists played that bunch of kids on the Copacabana beach at dawn. We got hammered about six-nil. Two of the Press guys spent the entire evening chatting up a couple of Amazons in the nightclub. Remember? Went back with them to their apartment and ran for their lives when they found they were gay guys in drag.

And how about that party the Press threw for the team at the end of our three-match tour the summer before last. It was in a dump of a hotel in Moscow. We made such a racket that the hotel manager sent for the police. Two uniformed officers came to the room and they left three hours later. Completely legless. A couple of the Fleet Street guys have still got their police hats as souvenirs.

I'll never forget pulling a girl in a nightclub in Copenhagen after one of your pals had spent all evening trying to get her to go to bed with him. It cost him a couple of bottles of champers, three hours of his time and he got nothing in return. Got his own back, though. My next match he gave me the worst write-up I've ever had.

As it happens I've always got on well with the media guys. Some of them are total idiots but on the whole they're a pretty responsible lot and some of them know more about football than the blind clowns running the game in this country. I think they'll take my book apart because I want to go in strong and give a true picture of football. But if they're honest, they will admit that I've had the guts to tell it as it is.

Something I would like to make clear in the book is that not all footballers are screw-crazy studs like me. Every team has one or two rams. Every team has a couple of heavy drinkers. Every team has its mad gamblers. Every team has its quiet, normal, intelligent guys like Winner Williams and every team has its thickheads like Ronnie Dicks and Roger Hart.

If you've got to hang labels on me, I like to think of myself as quiet and intelligent as well as being the stud of the team. Deep down, Ed, there's nothing I would like better than to fall in love and settle somewhere with one woman. But, God knows why, I just can't form an emotional attachment with anybody.

The nearest I've come to being in love – whatever that word means – was with a girl I met in New York last summer during United's tour. It was planned that I should link up with the United team after the end of the England tour. I reached the hotel two hours ahead of the United team. Met this girl in the bar. Her name was Jane. She was built and looked like Diana Ross. Black and beautiful. Worked as a secretary to an ambassador in the United Nations. She had an apartment just off Broadway. I didn't surface from there for four days. United fined me £500. It was worth every penny.

I shall try to link up with her again when I join the Comets but I don't suppose it will be the same. She seemed to *understand* me better than any girl I've been with before or since. I told her about what happened in Fairmount and d'you know what she did? She cried. That's the sort of feeling she had. She really got through to me emotionally as well as physically.

There have been plenty of times when girls have staked emotional claims on me. But I've not been able to reciprocate. It seems to me that I've got no capacity for love. Elizabeth Rhodes, the wife of the TV chat show bore Harvey Rhodes, came up with the analysis that I'm too much in love with myself to spare any for anybody else.

Maybe she's right. I don't know. There's no danger of any emotional entanglement between Liz and me. She likes to screw. Full stop. She's been round here to the flat about a dozen times. We have a great understanding. Intellectually she leaves me dead, but we really hit it off physically. Let's face it,

Harvey Rhodes is as big a ram as me. So why shouldn't she get it wherever she can? I'm only too happy to supply her needs.

Only one other bird has got through to me on an emotional level and what a disillusionment that affair became. D'you remember when I nipped off to Majorca in mid-season with Miss Great Britain in tow? We'd had two dates during which we got on marvellously and found we had a lot in common. The crazy thing is that each time I took her home to her apartment I was dismissed with a kiss on the cheek. She agreed to come to Majorca with me on the spur of the moment and naturally I thought I'd cracked it. It turned out the bitch only came with me for the publicity. Would you believe she turned out to be a lesbian? What a waste.

I've recently had two nasty experiences with married women. They're the ones that give me most trouble. One of them is appropriately married to a *vice*-chairman. She's a raving nympho. I dropped her when she started talking about divorce from her husband and marriage to me. If you mention this in the book, Ed, disguise it as much as possible. George Stoughton would sue us both for all that we've got if he could identify his wife.

The other problem woman is the one who is bugging me right now and is the reason I'm awake making this tape instead of sleeping in the sack. She's a player's wife whose name I must keep to myself. Her husband has got a bad drink problem. She did all the chasing and wanted to tie in with me permanently. No way. I've had to tell her tonight that there's nothing doing and to get the hell out of it. She's a fabulous A-class screw but I want her in New York with me like I want a hole in the head.

Anyway, Ed, I've talked myself into tiredness which was the object of the exercise. Hope I've given you some more material for the book about the *real* Jackie Groves. I can't wait to read it . . .

Transcript of Tape-recording No. 3 Ends

6

EDDIE SIMMS was sitting listening to the tape I had recorded in the middle of the night. Every now and again he would scribble a shorthand note on to his pad and then listen as attentively as if he were tuned into a classical music concert. He laughed out loud at my description of the swimming pool incident.

'I was on the other side of the glass,' he said. 'Two of the great-grandfathers from the Football Association committee were sitting with me. They nearly had apoplexy. "That swimmer looks just like young Groves," one said. The other old boy changed from his reading glasses to his outdoor glasses and studied you as if you were some sort of giant fish in an aquarium. "By George, it is the Groves boy," he spluttered. "How dare he make such an exhibition of the England team!"'

Eddie was now convulsed with laughter at the memory but

controlled himself long enough to add: 'The other old boy then said, " We'll 'ave to report t'lad to the manager for this. 'E should have his England uniform on like t'rest of us." '

As Eddie re-ran the tape to listen to the section he had drowned out with his infectious laughter, I glanced through the newspapers he had brought with him. They all carried short front-page stories about United's denial that I was about to be sold to the Comets with cross-references to the sports page coverage of last night's match. Ask any footballer whether he reads newspaper reports of the games he plays in and the odds are that he will say 'no'. And the odds are that he is lying. Few of us can resist reading about ourselves, particularly if we know we have had a good game. I rarely agree with what's written but at least I try to understand the pressure the reporter was under when he wrote the report. I've sat in Press boxes with football writers during matches and am astonished they manage to make any sense of the action at all. A lot of them are screaming down telephones trying to make themselves heard for much of the game.

This is when they are writing what they call their running reports, describing the action as it happens for the early editions. Then within half an hour of the final whistle at an evening match they have to start dictating their considered reports for the big city editions. The differences between the descriptions of one match are often amazing.

Eddie looked over my shoulder as I finished the last report. 'Which goal description shall I include in the " What The Papers Say " chapter?' he asked.

I shrugged. ' I'll leave it to you,' I said. 'They've all been kind to me. The version that mentioned dad grabbed my old heart strings a bit; I would have loved him to have seen me score that goal. He was the first person to show me how to back-heel a ball.'

Eddie had the tape cassette in his hand. 'All right if I take this back to my office and get it transcribed?'

'Be my guest. It would be pointless me making the recording if you're not going to note down what I say. I want this to be my book as much as possible, Ed. I had one published in my name three years ago. Remember it? It was called *Rootin' Tootin' Jackie Groves*. I think I saw the ghost-writer twice. He did it nearly all from cuttings. That was when I broke with my agent. I wanted somebody representing me who was interested in more than just seeing he got his ten per cent.'

There seemed to be something bothering Eddie. I had known him long enough to realize that when he started nervously patting down the bush of fair hair that sprouted in the middle of his forehead he was preparing to ask a difficult question.

'Come on, Ed,' I encouraged, 'spit it out. What's sticking in your throat?'

He forced a smile. 'For a bone-headed footballer, you're quite perceptive.' He paused and then finally made the point that was worrying him. 'It's to do with the problem you're having with the player's wife. You know, the one you talk about on the tape.'

Now it was my turn to force a smile. 'What is it, Ed? D'you think I've given her too high a rating?'

Eddie didn't even make a pretence at a smile. 'Fleet Street's overflowing with rumours about you and Billy Willson's wife,' he said hurriedly, as if he would feel better once the words were out. 'A freelance photographer who lives somewhere around here has seen her leave your apartment a couple of times. The second time he photographed her.'

'What is he, a peeping fucking Tom?'

'At least two of the Sunday papers are trying to follow it up,' Eddie continued, talking across my sudden anger. 'They just might be publishing something this weekend. I've been tapped for information but I told them to piss off. Anyway, as it happens I don't know anything about it.'

I was losing a battle to control my temper. 'What's it got to do with Fleet Street, for fuck's sake?' I said, raising my voice as if Eddie was their representative. 'What I do in my bed is my business. I can screw who I like when I like. It only concerns me and the person I happen to be banging at the time.'

Eddie's mouth moved but no words came out. I was into my stride and was not going to be interrupted. 'I just happen to know that one of the gentlemen whose football match report I've just read is balling our manager's secretary,' I said. 'Good luck to him. That's his business. You told me just last week that one of your former editors is screwing his secretary between editions. Good luck to him. Why shouldn't I be allowed to screw anybody I please and who pleases me without muck-raking reporters playing the part of voyeurs?'

Eddie sank down into an armchair, deflated and unusually miserable. 'I'm not here to debate Fleet Street ethics, Jackie,' he said, quietly but with some force. 'Yesterday you admitted that Fleet Street was interested in you because you're not, and I quote, "Virgin teetotal Jackie Groves". You've insisted on flaunting your sex life in the face of the public for three or more years now. If Fleet Street can pin down the fact that you're laying the captain's wife in the most momentous week in United's history, then surely to God you've got to admit that's one belter of a story. Like it or not, you are public property by the very nature of your life-style and your role in football as a controversial yet gifted entertainer. Publicity seekers can't pick and choose what is written about them.'

Now I was sitting down. It was mid-day and I was still in my dressing-gown and pyjamas. I would feel better after a shower but at this moment I was nose-diving back into the sort of depression I had woken up to at 2.30 that morning.

'Sorry I got mad at you, Ed,' I said, knowing my apology would be quickly accepted and my loss of temper just as quickly forgotten. 'What should I do? I can't go round admitting to the world that I've been balling the captain's wife.'

Eddie was now composed and thinking straight for me. 'What would Jennie Willson say if a reporter asked her if she'd been having an affair with you?' he questioned.

I laughed at the picture that sprang to my mind. 'I reckon

Jen's first reaction would be to lay her tongue to the full vocabulary of the Glasgow gutter language. She hates reporters like poison, you know. She wouldn't admit a thing to them.'

'You don't know how these foot-in-the-door news reporters work,' said Eddie, looking concerned. 'They might show her a picture of her leaving this flat, or say that you've confessed the affair for money. How would she respond to that sort of approach?'

It was a bit early in the day but I was moved to mix myself a large drink. 'I guess I'll have to talk to Jennie first,' I said from the direction of the cocktail cabinet. 'Drink?'

Eddie shook his head and I returned to my seat, twirling the ice in my glass as my mind whirled trying to think of a way round what could boil up into a really nasty situation. Recalling Jennie's exit in the night, there was no knowing which way she would bounce.

'Has Billy had any wind of what's been going on?' Eddie asked, breaking into a grin when he saw the pained expression on my face.

'I'm still here in one piece,' I said, in no way meaning to be funny. 'That should answer your question. As you will have realized listening to my tape, Billy's really been hitting the bottle. Between you and me, there is little future in their marriage but I don't think even Billy knows it. He's too busy drinking himself stupid. If he carries on this way, I think United will kick him out before the start of next season. He has been embarrassing them a lot lately with his drunkenness.'

Eddie looked at his watch. 'Ouch, it's gone twelve,' he said.

'What happens now? D'you lose your glass slipper or something?'

He gave that pleasant smile of his. 'No, but I've got to be on my bike. I'm lunching with the publisher at one. I'll keep my ear to the ground in the Street and let you know if I hear any more on the Jennie Willson front. Meantime, I think you would be wise to have a quiet word with her. If you both deny it, I doubt that the Sundays have got anything strong enough to go on.'

I waited until Eddie had gone and then telephoned the Willson home. Billy Willson's unmistakable Aberdeen voice boomed in my ear. I replaced the receiver and retired to the shower room.

I was lying on the massage table. Not in Soho but in the United medical room. Dusty Rhodes was massaging life back into muscles that had stiffened following the previous night's match against Wanderers. I had telephoned him after my shower and he had agreed to wait at the ground for me.

'Saw your goal on the box late last night,' said Dusty, glad to have somebody to talk to after a night of despair worrying about his controversial sending-off by Marshall Twerp. 'It was a bit special. Right out of yer dad's book.'

'You couldn't give me higher praise than that, Dusty,' I said, grimacing with a mixture of pain and pleasure as he kneaded my back muscles with his 'magic' hands.

'Mind you,' he added, 'there was no way yer could 'ave got away with that goal a few years ago. Blimey, in me and yer dad's time we'd 'ave 'ad our legs kicked up in the air before we could 'ave 'ad 'alf a chance to do that pretty back-heel bit. 'Course, nowadays defenders ain't allowed to tackle from behind. But it was a bit special just the same.'

He was now working on my leg muscles and I was happy to lie there and let him drift into one of his 'all our yesterdays' moods, nodding in all the right places as he went back into a past he had never wanted to leave.

'Me and yer dad had some grand times together,' he said, laughing at some corked-up memory. 'We often used to room together on England trips and when we travelled away with United. 'Course, in them days we only got seventeen nicker a week. Not like now. Blimey, you boys spend for one round of drinks what we used to earn for a week's work. But we got more fun and enjoyment out of the game. More fun and enjoyment. Money's poisoned it all, y'see. Poisoned it.

'Look at that Animal Smith last night,' he went on. 'Could 'ave killed somebody, he could 'ave. And why? For the money. The players of both sides were on ten grand a man. Stands to reason that the boots are going to be flying with that sort of lolly around. Me and yer dad didn't earn that much in our entire career, son. Just think on that fact. Not in our entire career. Mind you, we used to 'ave some hard nuts in our day even though there weren't much money to be earned. I'm finking of blokes like Jimmy Scoular of Portsmouth, Roy Hartle of Bolton and Stan Lynn of Aston Villa. And when I was a kid I used t'stand on the terraces at Arsenal watching Wilf Copping mowing down opponents with tackles that would 'ave put a tank out of action. The difference was that these blokes were all fair about it. They were hard as nails but played within the rules. Look at 'em now. It's all shirt tugging, ankle tapping, behind-the-back-of-the-ref stuff. We learnt it all from the continentals. Worse day's work for British football was when we started taking more interest in European Cups than our own championship. And cor blimey, look at us now. Now it's the bleedin' Anglo-American Cup. I know you're an American by birth and all that, son, but I wish your lot would stick to baseball and that funny rugby game they play ...'

Dusty's voice was trailing off in the distance as I started to doze, my tired mind trying to catch up on sleep lost the night before. I was suddenly jerked wide awake by the ringing of the medical room wallphone.

'Who the bleedin' hell wants me now,' grumbled Dusty as he wiped his hands on a towel and walked to the telephone.

'No peace for the incestuous,' I said, stealing an Eddie Simms line. Dusty shot me a dirty look.

'Medical room,' he growled into the phone. Then he looked across at me. 'It's for you, lover boy. A BBC secretary wants to talk to you. Shall I tell the switch to put her through?' I nodded and, reluctantly dragging myself off the massage table, walked in the nude to the wallphone. The voice in my ear belonged to Jennie Willson. She sounded chillingly cold.

'I've got to talk to you,' she snapped. 'I shall be at your flat at seven o'clock this evening. Be there.'

The line went dead. Now my mind was in desperate need of a massage.

7

JENNIE WILLSON's hands trembled as she lit a cigarette. I poured her a brandy without asking. She looked in need of one.

'Fleet Street have found out,' she said, pulling deeply on her cigarette to stop herself from crying. 'About us.'

I handed her the glass and arranged myself in the seat opposite, my hands cradled round a large brandy. I was also in need of one.

'I know they have,' I said. 'How did . . .?'

She looked as if I had just slapped her around the face. 'What d'you mean "you know they have"?' she interrupted, struggling to get the words out. 'Why the hell didn't you tell me?'

'Only found out this morning. Called you at your home but he answered. I wasn't going to tell him, was I? How did you find out?'

'I had a worm of a reporter from one of the Sundays on the doorstep just after lunch. Thank God, Billy was sleeping off a lunchtime drinking session. He said they were going to publish a story about what he called "our friendship". Wanted to know whether I had any comment to make.'

I chuckled. 'The mind boggles.'

'It's nothing to laugh at, you juvenile bastard,' she snapped, her nerves at breaking point. 'You do realize what Billy will do to both of us if he finds out?'

She paused while we both considered the prospect of having Billy's shovel-sized fists thumping into our bodies. On my memory screen I saw him picking up two sailors in a nightclub in Amsterdam and smashing their heads together. He was a violent man by nature. I could think of better prospects than having him unloading punches on me.

'So what did you tell the reporter?' I asked, her nervousness begining to make me feel unsettled.

'I said he'd better leave immediately or I would call my husband,' she said. 'It was the first thing that came into my head. The reporter seemed quite nervous.'

The thought crossed my mind that I, too, would be nervous if Billy Willson was about to be called to remove me from his doorstep. The United fans had a chant that summed up Billy's fearsome power:

> He's six foot five
> And just as wide
> Here comes Billy Willson
> To eat you alive.

Jennie gulped in another mouthful of tobacco. She looked ready to eat the cigarette. 'He said you were talking openly about our affair,' she added. 'I had to make up my mind on the spot whether he was lying. I decided to call his bluff and said, "In that case I will not only sue your paper but Jackie Groves as well for spreading malicious lies." Then I slammed the door in his face. It took me about an hour to track you down to the ground. Now what are we going to do?'

I drained my brandy glass, hoping to find an answer at the bottom. I decided to play it hard. 'We can deny everything quite happily following your exit last night,' I said. 'It's true to say there's nothing between us.'

'You bastard,' she said.

'Provided we don't see each other again and we both keep our mouths shut, I don't see what Fleet Street can do about it. They've got nothing to go on apart from a snatched picture of you leaving this flat. They would want a lot more evidence than that before risking printing anything about us.'

'Jackie Groves triumphs again,' she sneered. 'Whose wife will it be next? You've kicked Pam Stoughton out. Now me. What about Mrs Turner? The chairman's wife is what you would call "a bit of a goer". Why not get your cock into her?'

I returned to the cocktail cabinet and poured myself a second brandy. She had only taken a sip from her glass. 'This time next week, Jen, I'll be over in the States,' I said, controlling myself well considering the provocation. 'I'll be out of your hair and what's happened between us will just be history. Then you can try to put together the pieces of your marriage again. I didn't come between you and Billy. It was booze. Perhaps if you started showing him more attention you might find whatever you had when you first married him.'

'Don't you dare preach to me, you pompous little shitbag,' she shouted through a sudden flood of tears.

One thing I hate is the sight and sound of women crying. It always makes me feel helpless and guilty. I made a wrong move by beginning to show her sympathy. 'Come on, Jen,' I said, sitting on the arm of her chair and resting her head on my thigh. 'We've had some good times together. Don't let it end like this.'

She put her arms up and clung to me as if I was a lifebelt. 'All the women you've been with . . . you still don't understand them, do you,' she said through a succession of sobs. 'Don't you realize I'm in love with you? I don't want to go back to Billy. I want to stay with you. Go to New York with you.'

My mood of helplessness was suddenly overtaken by one of self-preservation. I unhitched myself from her arms and started pacing the room. 'We went through all this last night, Jen,' I pleaded. 'What the fuck do I know about love? I don't want to solo it with any woman. Ever.'

I turned and faced her as I delivered my final word to make sure she received it loud and clear. 'Let me say it once more, Jen, so that you understand me good. There is no way I want you in New York with me. Whatever we've had going for us is finishing right here and now. Now for God's sake go home to Billy. He needs you. I don't.'

It was as if I had pressed a launching button. She leapt off the chair sobbing, picked up her handbag and ran to the front door. Concerned that she might do something daft like run under a bus, I chased her to the door to try to calm her. As I attempted to pull her back into my apartment, we were both momentarily blinded by the flash of a photographer's bulb. With his prized picture on film, he raced off down the stairs and out of sight.

Fleet Street now had enough evidence to go ahead and publish the scandal of Jackie Groves and the captain's wife. Charming. Fucking charming.

Transcript of Tape-recording No. 4

GROVES: I'm bombed out of my mind, Ed. So would you be if you had my problems. What do I do? What the fuck do I do? That ponce of a peeping Tom photographer snatched a picture of Jennie and me together a couple of hours ago. Just as I'd sorted her out. We'd ended it. It was all over. Nothing to write about. Now they've got a picture of us together and the story will be all over one of the Sundays. . . .

He's six foot five
And just as wide
Here comes Billy Willson
To eat me alive.

My first thought, Ed, and you'll be disgusted with me for this, was to piss off. Run away. Take off. Anywhere – America, Spain – anywhere the first plane took me. I don't mind admitting I'm shit scared of that maniac Billy Willson. Who wouldn't be? But what would running away do? What would it solve? In the past I've always got myself in trouble by being impulsive. This time I've sat down and tried to think things out properly. I hope you're proud of me for that, Ed. My dad would have been, you know. It's because of him I'm not running away.

I always promised him that one day I'd play on the *real* Wembley. Remember the Wembley I told you about in Fairmount? Well Saturday's my one and only chance to keep that promise. All my England matches have been on away grounds. Now at last I can get to play on the ground that meant so much to dad. I can't run out on him.

It's taken nearly a bottle of brandy before I've arrived at the decision not to run off. Even started packing my bags. Hope I don't run out of courage in the morning when the booze wears off. At least this'll help sell the book, Ed. Mind you, if Billy Willson gets his hands on me it will have to be published postu ... poshtum ... pothumous ... oh, hell, Ed, you know what I mean ...

. . . Morning, Ed. I've just showered an almighty hangover out of my head. I've been listening to what I taped last night and you'll be pleased to know that I haven't run out of courage. At least, not yet. You never know, with luck Billy won't get to know about Jen and me until Sunday. It shouldn't be so difficult to avoid him then.

I shall drop this tape in at your office on my way to the training ground this morning. Can you do some detective work for me in Fleet Street and see if they're going ahead with the story about Jen and me? How about this for an idea: is it remotely possible that the photographer would sell his film to me instead of to a newspaper? I'd pay him a grand for it. That way Fleet Street would have nothing to go on. They could build something up around a picture of Jen and me together. Particularly as she was bawling her head off at the time the photograph was taken. But without the picture I can't see how they can print a story of any substance.

Incidentally, while I was in the shower I thought of another anecdote you might want to fit into the book. What brought it back to me was getting pissed out of my mind on brandy. Last time I did that was in Norway last season. It was on the eve of a UEFA Cup tie. We knew it would be an easy game and treated the trip as a mini-vacation.

We bought duty-free liquor on the way out and I drank right through the night with my hotel room-mate. It was Billy Willson. We were both so drunk that we missed our breakfast call the next morning. Scott Ryder came to our room and his nose quickly told him what we'd been up to. The place smelt like a distillery. He ordered us to stay in our beds and said he would speak to us later in the day.

The rest of the team went off for a training session and Billy and I slept on until about lunchtime. Ryder came to see us as we were coming back to the land of the sober and told us we were dropped from the team. He said that to protect the good name of the club he would tell the Press that we had both been confined to our room with a stomach bug. We were both fined £100 and Ryder said if the real reason why we had missed the match got into the newspapers he would make it £1,000 each. You're the first person outside the club to be told the story.

Must go now, Ed. There's somebody ringing the door-bell ...

Transcript of Tape-recording No. 4 Ends

There were two guys at the door. I didn't like the look of either of them. They stood shoulder to shoulder as if practising to build a defensive wall.

'Sorry to trouble you so early in the morning, Jackie,' one of them said, clearly not sorry at all. 'Wanted to catch you before you went training.'

'We're from the *Sunday Herald*,' the other one announced. 'We'd like to discuss a deal with you that could earn you a lot of money.' I smelt rats. 'What sort of deal have you got in mind?' I asked, with a strong suspicion of what the answer would be.

'Can we come in for a quick chat?' the first one asked. 'We won't keep you long.'

I looked down at my watch. 'Sorry you guys,' I said, taking a turn at not feeling sorry at all. 'I'm running late for training as it is.'

Now the second reporter took charge. 'We have been authorized by our office to offer you five thousand pounds for just a little assistance on a story we've been working on,' he said from behind an oily smile. 'We would just like your brief comments on your, uh, association with Mrs Jennifer Willson, the wife of the United captain.'

This is what I'd expected but it still arrived like a punch to the throat. 'My brief comment is no comment,' I snarled, jerking at the door to slam it in their face. I got it as far as reporter number one's foot. So this is what Eddie meant by the foot-in-the-door methods.

'If you'll give us just a short, signed statement we shall raise our offer to £7,500,' said number two. 'All we want is . . .'

I didn't let him finish. 'All I want is for you two gutter rats to fuck off,' I said, my temper out of control.

'Don't be like that, Jackie,' said number one, his foot standing up well to the pressure I was putting on the door. 'We're going to publish the story anyway, old boy, so you might as well make a few bob out of it.'

'After all, we've even got a picture of the two of you together,' said number two just a split second before my right fist smashed against his nose.

They both back-pedalled like full-backs under attack.

'Thanks for giving us a few more paragraphs to go with our story,' said number one, dropping a calling card on the landing. 'If you change your mind about the £7,500, here's my number at the *Herald*.'

Number two had a rapidly reddening handkerchief to his nose. 'Enjoy the game on Saturday, Jackie,' he said as he followed number one to the stairs. 'And enjoy reading our story on Sunday.'

I slammed the apartment door shut. As I collected my training bag, I wondered whether I should have run away after all.

8

HUGH BLACKLEY had missed his vocation. He should have been a torture expert with the Gestapo. His training schedules, even this late in the season, were designed to drive the players to the edge of exhaustion. Today he was pushing us over the edge.

I had driven to the training ground with my mind reeling from the events and booze of the past two days. After dropping the tape cassette into Eddie's office I once again sparred with the idea of pointing my Lotus Éclat in the direction of Heathrow Airport but decided that for once in my life I had to face up to a crisis. Running away would merely delay the inevitable explosion.

It was with a false bravado that I walked into the locker-room as if I didn't have a care in the world. The first person to confront me was Billy Willson. I braced myself, ready to use my leather hold-all as a defensive weapon.

'Christ, Jackie, you look like I feel,' he said, smacking me on the back with a huge open hand. 'I'm just coming out of a bender. I've been permanently pissed since we won the championship.'

The pin was back in the grenade. I laughed out loud, as much a release of tension as amusement at Willson's comment. Obviously he had not yet been given a sneak preview of the *Sunday Herald* exclusive.

'Late again, Grovesie,' was the familiar welcoming growl from Hugh Blackley. 'You've missed my little chat to the lads. What I had to say applies particularly to you. This will be our last day's hard training before Saturday's Final. I'm going to run the piss out of all of you and from today on I want you all to stay sober until after the game at Wembley. There's time enough for celebrating.

'There is enormous prestige at stake when we meet your blood brothers from the colonies on Saturday, as well as the bonus that each of us is on if – or should I say, *when* – we win. So I don't want any of you sabotaging the team effort by hitting the bottle or being over-active in bed. Do I make myself clear?'

I was still high on the relief of not having been beaten to a pulp by Willson and was content to nod my obedience to Blackley who was clearly practising for when he was finally able to bury the knife deep enough into Scott Ryder's back to take over as manager.

He had his manager's voice and manner switched on and I was so happy to still be in the land of the living that I surrendered myself to his insane training programme. I was just being sick for a second time after ninety minutes of knackering repetition runs when I spotted two familiar figures standing among a small knot of spectators on the trackside.

They stood shoulder to shoulder as if still practising to build a defensive wall. It was number one and number two from the *Sunday Herald*.

I retched again. This time it was from fear rather from exhaustion.

The two reporters were waiting for me when I came out of the dressing-room. I was in a hurry to get to the ground where Hugh Blackley told me Scott Ryder wanted to see me urgently. I also wanted to get the hell away from Billy Willson as quickly as possible.

'Just wanted to apologize for this morning's little episode,' said number one, dropping in step beside me as I hurried towards my car. Number two kept a respectful distance.

'Have you thought any more about our offer?' number one added, studying me anxiously for any signs of physical reaction.

Two schoolboys stood barring the way to my car door, holding out autograph books like beggars with bowls. I signed them with an automatic reflex action of my right hand, my mind on what answer to give the snotty *Sunday Herald*'s representative rather than a signature that I had scrawled thousands of times before.

I decided on bluff tactics. 'Here's a quote for you to take back to your editor,' I said, ushering the two schoolboys gently to one side out of hearing range. Number one held a small pocket tape-recorder close to my chin. 'I am at this moment on my way to see my lawyer – sorry, solicitor – about slanderous things that have been said to me by two *Sunday Herald* reporters. If one word appears in that newspaper about anything to do with my private life, I shall sue for more money than there is in the whole of Fleet Street. End quote.'

Number one played his ace. 'In that case, Jackie,' he said, 'we shall discuss the matter with Billy Willson and see what light he can shed on it.'

I slid behind the wheel of my car and before shutting the door tried one more bluff. 'I've told Billy the action I'm taking and he is right behind me,' I called in the direction of number one. 'You can discuss it with him now if you want but I think I should warn you that he is in a bone-breaking mood.'

Number one moved quickly to the side of his colleague out of the way of my car as I gunned the engine to life. He obviously feared that I might run him down. The thought did rear its head but I squashed it. As I drove out of the car park I watched the two reporters in earnest conversation in my rear-view mirror. I was gambling on them not having enough facts about Jennie and me to be able to approach her husband. They had a snatched picture of the two of us together but what did that really prove?

If they had been so sure of their facts there was no way they would have come back to see me so quickly. All they had to go on was the word and no doubt fuzzy picture of a hungry freelance photographer out to make a quick buck for himself.

As I waited to join the traffic moving past the training ground, I was relieved to see numbers one and two move to their car. I was, temporarily at least, off the hook.

Scott Ryder was walking in ever-decreasing circles in the car park at the United ground when I pulled into the players' section. He looked like a man who had just been told he has a terminal disease.

I had hardly got the car door open before he was snapping and snarling at me as if I were his worst enemy. 'You seem determined to damage this club as much as you can before I can get you out,' he growled.

I looked at him as if he were mad, which at that precise moment he definitely was. 'What the fuck have I done now?' I asked, the swearing triggered by his aggressive approach.

'Don't use your gutter language to me,' he said. 'You seem to want to spend your whole life in the gutter. What's wrong with you, Jackie? Are you out of your mind?'

As I locked my car door I couldn't help but laugh, which made Ryder's face turn from grey to purple with anger. 'Me out of my mind?' I said. 'It's not me who's flipped my lid. If you would just tell me what you are all worked up about maybe I could understand what the hell's going on.'

Ryder pointed a finger towards the executive offices. 'I'll let the chairman tell you,' he barked. 'He's waiting to see you in the boardroom. But just let me tell you this, sonny. If you break the team spirit I've worked so hard to build up in this club then I'll break you.'

He marched off towards the boardroom, me following on behind in a state of total bewilderment. It entered my head that I should keep on walking right out of the ground and right out of England where I suddenly felt like an unwelcome foreigner, but a mixture of fear and curiosity lured me to the executive offices where John Turner was waiting with a greeting that was surprisingly warm and friendly. Once again I wondered if Ryder had gone off his head.

'Good t'see you, Jackie lad,' he boomed in a thick Yorkshire accent that had survived more than twenty years of mixing in the old boy network in the City where his wheeling and dealing with stocks and shares had earned him several million pounds and the grudging respect of the bowler-hatted brigade who looked on anybody from north of Watford as an invader from outer space. Turner had won control of United two years earlier after a bitter boardroom battle with the former chairman George Stoughton, who had been relegated to vice-chairman. They were sworn enemies. Turner was an unashamed dictator, making decisions with little deference to the rest of the Board members, three of whom were 'puppet' directors that he had brought into the club in return for pledges of total support and non-interference.

He led us into the boardroom and signalled for Ryder and myself to sit at the oval, highly-polished table that dominated the middle of the room. 'Would you like a drink, lad?' he asked, walking towards the cocktail bar in the far corner. 'I'm sure you could do with one after your hard training session. Non-alcoholic, of course.'

'A coke would be fine,' I said, my mouth parched by the sudden tension generated by Ryder's outburst in the car park.

'How about you, Scott?' Turner asked as he deftly prised

the top off a bottle of coke with a bottle opener made in the shape of a footballer wearing United colours.

Ryder controlled his thirst for Scotch. 'Just a ginger ale, Mr Chairman, if you've got one,' he said, unaware that his worsening drinking habits were the talk of the club.

Turner poured himself a treble Scotch and soda, handed the glasses round and then sat in the large leather-padded chair at the top of the table.

'That was a great goal Monday night, lad,' he said, staring into his glass as if he could see an action-replay picture reflected in the drink. 'Aye, a great one. I was hoping to congratulate you, personal like, after the match but you were off like t'great north wind.'

'I've never been one for hanging around after matches,' I replied, wondering what the hell this was all leading up to.

'Your dad would have been proud of that goal. Reet proud. I saw him score one like that back in about 1954 for England against Scotland. He went round bloody centre-half as if he were a statue and whoosh, the ball were in back of t'bloody net before the goalkeeper could move. D'you remember that goal, Scott?'

'I was the statue, Mr Chairman,' Scott said without a flicker of a smile. He had won thirty caps with Scotland.

Turner laughed like a hyena. 'That's bloody reet,' he said between gasps of laughter that brought red blotches to the cheeks of his bloated, hard drinker's face. 'Bet you thought of Jackie's dad Monday, eh? It was a reet belter of a goal.'

I shifted uncomfortably on my leather seat, sensing that I was about to hear just why I had been summoned to the boardroom.

The chairman used a pocket handkerchief to wipe tears away from his eyes. 'I'll tell you what, Jackie,' he said, his laughter now giving way to a serious mood, 't'reason your dad enjoyed his football so much in those days was because there were a wonderful team spirit. Aye, a wonderful team spirit in the dressing-room and on t'pitch at club and country level. There's never been a successful team without good team spirit. I put team spirit up there at the top of t'list of ingredients for success along with skill and tactics. Aye, right at top.'

He poured half his drink down his throat in one shot, placed his glass on the table and then leaned forward as if he was going to take me into his confidence. 'My ambition, lad, is t'make United into the greatest club in the world,' he said, his eyes shining like an evangelist's in full voice. 'Monday, it were the League championship which takes us into t'European Cup next season. Saturday, it will be the Anglo-American Cup. Second only in importance to t'European Cup. I know this is only t'first Anglo-American Final but t'eyes of the world will be on Wembley. It's the new world versus the old and it's vital for t'prestige of this club and this country that we win.'

I could almost hear 'Land of Hope and Glory' in the background. 'We've got the skill and the tactics to beat the Comets,' he continued. 'But have we got the necessary team spirit, lad? That's what we must ask ourselves. Have we got the team spirit?'

Just as I was about to make a token reply, Turner's eyes suddenly hardened. 'Is it true you're poking Billy Willson's missus?' he asked, throwing the question across the table like a dart at the bull's eye.

For a second I could get no words out. I looked at Ryder who was slumped in his seat like a beaten fighter in his corner. 'What's that got to do with anybody?' I at last managed to blurt out.

Turner stood up and started to pace the room. 'It's got everything to do with team spirit,' he said. 'A player laying another player's wife behind his back, that's bad for team spirit. Nothing could be worse.'

Now I understood why Ryder was so angry. A strict Scottish Presbyterian, he could accept a lot of things but this sort of infidelity was beyond his understanding and forgiveness.

'Look, Mr Turner, what I do in bed is my business,' I said, leaning heavily on the argument I had used with Eddie Simms. 'I remember you paying a hooker £100 for a lay after one of our matches in Manchester ...'

It was Ryder's turn to get to his feet. 'You've got a disgusting mouth, Groves,' he snarled. 'Apologize to the chairman immediately.'

Turner put an arm round Ryder's shoulder and steered him towards the door. 'Let me handle this please, Scott,' he said in an almost fatherly tone. 'You go back to your office and get on with your work. I'm sure you've got a lot on your plate this week. I'll talk to you later.'

Ryder walked heavily out of the room and Turner locked the door behind him. He went to the cocktail bar with his glass and poured himself another large Scotch and then returned to his chair.

He settled himself and then fixed me with a stare and gave a half smile. 'Sorry about Ryder, lad,' he said. 'Wish I'd never told him what I wanted t'see you about. I had two reporters round at my office this morning from a Sunday rag. Said they were working on information that you were having an affair with Billy Willson's wife. I told them it was none of my business and certainly none of their business.'

I finished off the coke to moisten my throat ready for my say but he talked through my attempt to interrupt. 'But it is my business, Jackie. Because, like I say, it's all about team spirit. Look, lad, I'm not old fashioned like Scott Ryder. He'd be happy to see sex abolished and thinks women should still be fitted with chastity belts. But there's a right time, a right place and the right woman for it. A team-mate's wife is not the right woman.'

He took a cigar case from an inside pocket and lit a six-inch Havana after snipping at the end with a gold cutter. He rolled the cigar around between his thumb and two fingers as if seeking the most comfortable holding position. 'I'll tell you something, Jackie lad,' he said, jabbing the cigar in my direction, 'it's breaking my heart that we are letting you go to the Comets. You are without a shadow of a doubt the most skilful footballer we've got in this country. But t'reason I'm having to let you go lad is that you let your cock rule your brain and that's going to destroy you.

'As the chairman of this great club I get to hear what all my staff are up to. I know that Billy Willson is pouring gallons down his throat and I could tell you exactly how much Scotch t'manager's drinking in his office every day. I know which turnstile operators are on t'fiddle. And I'll have them, don't you fret. I also know about the private lives of my players. You, for instance, lad. I knew a year ago that you were giving George Stoughton's wife a seeing to.

'I let that one go. That daft bastard's getting what he deserves. But this nonsense with Billy Willson's wife has got to stop right now.'

He paused for a drink and at last I had a chance to get a word in. 'It's over and finished,' I said quickly before he could get started again. 'There was nothing in it. Just straight sex.'

'But what about the papers, lad?' Turner asked from behind his fat cigar.

'I can't see that they've got enough to go on for a story they can print. A photographer snatched a picture of us together but it wasn't as if we were in bed or anything. We were both fully clothed and outside my front door.'

'The *Herald*'s one of Lord Brandon's rags,' he said, as much to himself as to me. 'I'll have a word with old Brandy. He owes me a few favours. Perhaps I can stop them printing anything. What does Billy Willson know about all this?'

I shrugged. 'Nothing, as far as I know, otherwise he would have torn me limb from limb by now.'

Turner was pouring himself another drink. He should talk about the drinking habits of Ryder and Willson! 'Scott Ryder's immediate reaction when I told him about you and Mrs Willson was that we should drop you from t'team Saturday,' he said. 'But I over-ruled him. And d'you know why, lad? Because I want to win this match so bad that it hurts. *You* can win it for us. I know you're a sensible lad when it comes to brass and it will earn you a bloody fortune in t'States if you can turn it on at Wembley. Aye, a bloody fortune. They'll all be watching it on telly over there and you can return home a bloody hero.'

We were both silent for a second as we conjured up pictures of a United victory at Wembley. The chairman was right. I could make a fortune in the United States by making myself a household name before I even started my career over there with the Comets. But most of all I wanted to be on a winning side at Wembley for my dad. I stood up and shook hands with the chairman. 'Thanks for your time and advice, Mr Turner,' I said, meaning it. 'I shall do my very best for you at Wembley on Saturday.'

He beamed from behind his cigar and walked to the door to unlock it. Just before twisting the key he turned and gave me that hard stare of his. 'One thing, lad,' he said, 'I want you to forget all about that prostitute in Manchester. We are all entitled to our little indiscretions provided it's not on our own doorstep. All right?'

'Right on,' I said with a smile. I wouldn't even mention it in my book.

The chairman was just steering me out into the corridor when the burly figure of George Stoughton came bustling towards us. He was obviously agitated.

'I've been trying to get hold of you for two bloody days, Turner,' he shouted from twenty yards away, making no attempt to disguise his contempt for the chairman.

Turner and I reversed back into the boardroom as Stoughton stormed in, waving a clutch of newspapers as if swatting a flight of flies. 'What's all this in the newspapers about you selling Jackie Groves?' he asked, tossing the papers down on to the boardroom table.

'Calm down, Stoughton,' advised Turner, with the sort of

tone a schoolmaster would use to an over-excited pupil. 'You'll burst a boiler.'

I tried to excuse myself but Stoughton put up a hand like a traffic cop halting a speeding vehicle. 'No, you stay here, Jackie,' he insisted. 'What I've got to say concerns you so you might as well stay and listen rather than hear a distorted version at some future date.'

Turner was at the bar pouring himself another large Scotch. He didn't invite Stoughton to join him. Composing himself in the large leather-padded chair at the top of the table, he stared up at the man he had replaced as chairman and challenged him with his eyes to try to shake his exaggerated mood of indifference.

'How much truth is there in these stories about you doing a deal with the Comets for Jackie's transfer?' Stoughton demanded to know.

The chairman pulled on his cigar, taking his time before answering. 'There's a board meeting here on Friday,' he said. 'I might be in a position to make a statement then.'

Turner's arrogance pumped Stoughton's blood pressure to boiling point. 'Who the hell do you think you are, Turner?' he shouted. 'You may be chairman but this isn't a one-man club, you know. I have poured too many years of sweat and blood into this place to stand by and see you destroy it with your Hitleresque megalomania.'

This triggered a loud chuckle from Turner, whose confidence was no doubt considerably strengthened by the fact that he held sixty per cent of the shares in United.

'I'm no lawyer, Stoughton,' he said, 'but I would think I could get a few bob out of you in court for that little slanderous outburst. Seeing as 'ow we won t'championship on Monday I can't see that any court would agree I'm destroying United.'

The chuckle had now been replaced by a sneer. 'Me destroying t'club?' he said with incredulity. 'When I took over from you as chairman we were 'alf a million in debt.

Now we're only a few thousand on the wrong side at t'bank and I'm going t'put that right very shortly.'

'If you mean by selling Jackie Groves, then I could get a court to agree that you're mad,' Stoughton argued. 'I'll organize the biggest protest movement you've ever seen if you go ahead with it. You may have the voting strength, Turner, but I'll make your name shit in this club if you let Groves go back to America. You've always resented the fact that it was me who signed him for this club.'

Turner laughed out loud. 'It's you whose lost your marbles, Stoughton,' he said. ''Ow can you stand there and claim t'credit for signing t'lad? A blind man could see he could play t'game like his dad before him.'

Stoughton looked to me for support. 'Tell him, Jackie,' he said, almost pleading. 'Tell him that it was me who persuaded you to join United.'

I wanted no part of their childish argument, but I couldn't miss this opportunity to prick Stoughton's vanity which had always irritated me ever since I first met him after my first-team début for the club. 'Sorry, Mr Stoughton, but I didn't need any persuading,' I said in all honesty. 'I chose United rather than United choosing me. I had made up my mind when I was a boy in America that this was the club I wanted to play for. If you have to give anybody the credit for actually signing me, I suppose you would have to say it was Scott Ryder.'

Stoughton's eyes glinted but he wouldn't give up. 'Who the hell do you think it was told Ryder to sign you?' he said. 'We had special progress reports on you from the age of sixteen. I insisted on seeing every one of them. There was no way I was going to allow another club near you. Now this maniac wants to let you go back to the States without even consulting the board.'

Turner, his face flushed by all the whisky he had consumed, suddenly stood up aggressively. 'One more crack about my sanity Stoughton, and I'll take the greatest pleasure in sticking my fist down your bloody throat,' he said, quickly returning to a sitting position before the vice-chairman could take him up on the challenge.

Like me, Turner obviously knew that Stoughton had been more than useful with his fists in his time. He was a motor dealer who had made his fortune in the hard competitive world of the used-car market. I had got to know all about his background during my screwing sessions with his wife, Pam, who told me how he boasted that in his youth he got a gang organized to smash a mob of protection racketeers threatening to put him out of business. Now he dealt only in the Rolls Royce end of the market and talked with an acquired accent that carried no trace of his East London background. He was now into his late fifties, thirty years older than Pam, who had been named as co-respondent in his divorce from his first wife.

The vice-chairman stood menacingly over Turner. 'Just give me a straight answer,' he demanded. 'Is it right you are negotiating to sell Groves to the Comets?'

I decided to speak up before their hatred for each other broke into violence. 'Have you considered the possibility that perhaps I would like to return to America?' I asked Stoughton, who backed away from Turner as if I had put the point of a sword to his chest.

'So it's true,' he said. 'You've arranged a deal behind the backs of the board. I'll see you regret this, Turner. You've given me the chance I've waited for to get you kicked out of the club.'

'You're talking out of your arse, as usual, Stoughton,' Turner said. 'I'll give you full details of what's 'appening at the board meeting on Friday and not before. When you hear the deal you'll shut your mouth and agree I'm doing what's best for United. I've already told t'lad here that it's in everybody's best interests that he goes before he destroys t'club and 'imself with his cock.'

Stoughton looked at me and shook his head like a doctor

deciding there was no hope of saving his patient. 'You're a great disappointment to me, Jackie,' he said, then turning and walking out of the boardroom with the heavy tread of a gambler just beaten in a shit-or-bust dice game.

Turner was pouring himself a celebratory drink. 'Thanks for your support, lad,' he said. 'That bastard Stoughton would do anything to get me out of this chair. If you had let him think you would like to stay here at United he would 'ave used it to turn the world against me. As it is, I'll get 'im voted to death at Friday's meeting.'

I wondered to myself what Stoughton's reaction to my transfer would have been had he known his wife had wanted to leave him to marry me.

George Stoughton and Billy Willson. I visualized for a moment what they could do to me between them. It was a horrendous thought.

As I left the boardroom and walked in a reflective mood to my car, I made a secret vow. 'From here on in,' I said to myself, 'married women are out ...'

9

EDDIE SIMMS was the greatest sitting-down darts player I have ever seen. His office was in a Dickensian building just off Fleet Street, a sparsely-furnished room lined with sports reference and record books and half filled by a huge mahogany desk scarred and stained with the initials and cigarette burns of a procession of previous occupants of the rented premises.

Suspended from a hook behind the door was Eddie's most treasured office possession. A dartboard. He had a swivel seat and could hit double top six times out of ten while spinning himself round like a human top. There were twelve darts on his desk in sets of three, all with different flight colours that represented Football League teams. His non-writing time was occupied playing the teams off against each other, victory going to the three darts with the highest score. It could be fairly disconcerting when you were being interviewed by him.

I had arrived from the United ground in the middle of a match between Spurs and Liverpool and Eddie refused to let my presence put him off. Dalglish had just hit the board to give Liverpool a treble nineteen when I asked Eddie if he'd had time to listen to the tape I had delivered on my way to training.

'Of course I've listened to it,' he said, suddenly swivelling and hurling Ardiles into the outer bull for a twenty-five for Spurs. 'Your speech was so slurred on the first half of the tape I thought my machine had gone wrong again. I see Billy Willson hasn't eaten you alive yet. Did you see him at training?'

As Eddie prepared to launch Heighway for Liverpool's final shot, I recounted the events since I had made the tape-recording. I gave him a description of the two *Sunday Herald* reporters, and noticed a sneer of contempt cross Eddie's face. Then I told him how I had been summoned to the United ground for the confrontation with Ryder and Turner.

Eddie threw Heighway with more force than usual and scowled when he recorded only seventeen, an eighth of an inch away from the treble wire. 'I apologize on behalf of Fleet Street for those two *Herald* rats,' he said. 'They are the dregs of our profession. They do all the sewer jobs for the *Herald*. Corringham and Mellor. You may recall their recent exposé of the television newsreader who is a transvestite. It was a very tasteful piece of reporting. Their intro read, "We've got news for you about John Barker. He's happiest when he is wearing women's clothes." Real Pulitzer Prize winning stuff.'

He spun and aimed the final dart of the match. Perryman scored a double top for Spurs to give them a 119–114 victory. Now I had Eddie's complete attention.

'I had a chat with a contact of mine at the *Herald* this morning,' he said. 'You undervalued that picture of you and Mrs Willson together. They've bought the photographer's film for five thousand pounds. Even if they can't get you or Mrs W. talking about your affair they are going to go ahead and use it on Sunday. Their most imaginative caption writer will cod something up about how the soccer superstar comforted the captain's wife in Cup Final week. It will be there for everybody to read between the lines that the pair of you have been at it.'

'How about if I sue them for invasion of privacy?' I asked, unable to disguise the desperation in my voice.

'There's nothing to stop you getting legal advice on that, Jackie,' he said, looking doubtful about the idea. 'But I've already told you that publicity seekers should learn to take it on the chin when suddenly they get unwanted attention. Supposing you were able to get a court injunction to stop the *Herald* publishing the picture, do you think that would arouse more public curiosity than if it were used? In no time at all everybody would know about you and Mrs Willson. That way you would not only have Billy Willson trying to eat you alive but also a gigantic legal bill to pay.'

I leaned forward from my wooden, straight-backed chair, selected a dart from the desk and threw it in a gesture of frustration at the board. It stuck in the outer rim and failed to score.

'Jackie Groves misses the target again,' said Eddie in a raised commentator's voice. 'These days, he scores only between the bed posts.'

He ducked my pretence at a punch and laughed. 'Cheer up, Jackie,' he said. 'Things can only get worse. What are your plans for the rest of the day? Have you got time for a taping session?'

'I've got to be at the television studio at seven,' I said, looking at my watch. 'So I've got five hours to waste before being confronted by that chatting loon Harvey Rhodes. I'd much rather be confronted by his wife.'

Eddie clapped his hands together. 'Great,' he said, with real enthusiasm. 'We'll get some soup and sandwiches in from the takeaway next door and then we can have a deeper dig into your past.'

He picked up a Nottingham Forest dart and hurled Trevor Francis at the board. It was a bull's-eye.

Transcript of Tape-recording No. 5

SIMMS: You are going to come out of this book with a shocking image, Jackie, and I would not want to defend you if somebody accused you of putting your cock before your career as a footballer. The question has to be asked, how much better a player would you be today if you lived a professional athlete's life off as well as on the pitch?

GROVES: Point number one, Ed. I don't give a damn about my image. What the hell is image anyway? That word has become the exclusive property of the media. They create the images of people in the public eye, pigeon-holing everybody under such crass titles as 'superstar', 'sex symbol', 'high living', 'playboy' and the one that makes me really puke when they write about me, 'football's most eligible bachelor'. Sometimes I wish the writers would choke on their clichés. It's my opinion, answering your question about my life off the pitch, that I wouldn't be half the player that I am if I lived the way, say, that Scott Ryder would like me to live. If I had to conform and become one of the sheep, I'm sure my football would suffer. I like the freedom to do things my way on and off the pitch. If I were repressed in my private life, I would be like a zombie when I played. I would become blinkered and lacking in imagination. There is an overload of straight up-and-down footballers in the English League who play with their legs and feet but not their minds. Individualists are too often crushed by bullying coaches who turn them into robots unable to think and act for themselves.

SIMMS: I'm not saying you should become one of the sheep. But surely all the screwing you do must drain something out of you. You've got to admit you take it to extremes. I mean, look at Monday with that girl Sally ...

GROVES: Surely that helps my case? All right, so I screwed

her a couple of hours before the game. Did it affect my performance on the pitch? As it happens, that wasn't my record. I once had a quickie in the back of the United bus with a girl who had been following me around for months. Smuggled her on to the bus and balled her on the back seat just forty-five minutes before a League game at Manchester. I scored our goal in a one-one draw.

It just happens, Ed, that I thrive on it. No doubt it would destroy many other players. Winner Williams, for instance. He tells me he wouldn't dream of touching his wife for at least forty-eight hours before a match because, and I quote Winner, 'intercourse saps the mind and the muscles'. Fine. That's what suits him. But I don't think not having it helps. If it did, the Vatican would have a world championship team. Better not put that in the book, Ed. I think it's all to do with your attitude of mind. If you are the sort who thinks screwing before a game is going to weaken you, then it will. If you're like me and you think a good bang will pep you up for a game, then it will. No two people are alike. You need a psychologist rather than a footballer to talk on this subject with any real depth.

Take your game, Ed. Writing. I was reading an article in an old copy of *Time* recently about Georges Simenon, the creator of Inspector Maigret and one of the most prolific novelists that has ever breathed. He reckoned he had screwed thousands of women during his life. I think he put the figure at more than ten thousand. It didn't affect his astonishing output as a writer, did it? Yet I wonder how you would react to such a procession of lays?

SIMMS: Bloody hell, it's all I can do to satisfy my missus.

GROVES: There you are then. It's all in the mind. You would no doubt fall asleep over your typewriter if you had a lay just before starting work. Simenon obviously thrived on it. Just like Jackie Groves. Mind you, I've got a long way to go before I'm in his league!

SIMMS: A media cliché coming up. You have the image of

being a playboy. Like it or lump it, you've got it. Now what interests me for the book is *when* you started to adopt your present lifestyle. I saw you make your début as an eighteen-year-old, fresh-faced kid and you looked then as if butter wouldn't melt in your mouth, if you'll excuse another cliché. Just reminisce for a few minutes on your early days with United.

GROVES: I was living with my mother and grandparents at Southgate when I made my United début. It was the house where mom had grown up. A semi-detached, three bedroomed place. Her dad had been headmaster at a school in North London. This was years ago. He's eighty-odd now but has still got a mind as sharp as a needle. I'm not his favourite grandson. Thinks I should conform. He believes all the world's troubles could be cured by bringing back capital punishment, conscription and the cane, in that order.

Anyway, as you know I hit it off straight away in the United first-team. Scored thirty-one First Division goals in my first full season and got into the England team when I was nineteen. I was given a new contract after a year that took my basic weekly wage up to £400. With bonuses, I was earning thirty thousand a year within two seasons of turning professional, plus another ten to fifteen thousand pounds from sponsorship, ghosted newspaper and magazine articles and endorsements.

At first, I was a little over-awed by the older professionals in the team. You've got to remember that I was realizing a lifetime's ambition by playing for United in the English League and I didn't want to spoil it by putting a foot wrong off the pitch. So I went along with what the majority of other players used to do. Afternoons I would go to the snooker hall and play for £20 a match. I was quite a hustler and they nicknamed me Minnesota Fats. But one day it was me who got hustled. That sly bastard Ronnie Dicks brought in a Cockney pal of his who needled me into playing him for a grand. I had beaten him four times out of five when it was

£20 a match but when the real bread went down he suddenly started potting the balls like Willie Mosconi. It was my break right at the start and after that I didn't get back to the table. There was a lot of side betting and Dicks and his crowd really cleaned up. From that day on I stayed away from the snooker hall. Pool was always my game, anyway.

SIMMS: How active was your sex life in those early days?

GROVES: It was as easy as picking apples off a tree. There were United groupies everywhere you turned. Slags, a lot of them. But I wasn't fussy. Trevor Beckett had an apartment in Chelsea and he and I used to screw ourselves silly there. That all ended of course when Trev had his accident. Worst moments of my life, those when the seriousness of Trev's injuries became clear. All right, he was drunk at the wheel of his car. Out of his head. But he didn't deserve that. Not a wheelchair existence for the rest of his life.

SIMMS: Do you keep in touch with Trevor?

GROVES: Tried to. But he just didn't want to know. Suddenly we had nothing in common and when I was in his company I know I just made him more morose about what had happened to him. A lot of people thought I was to blame for the crash, you know. I got threatening telephone calls and anonymous letters calling me all sorts of things. But I honestly only got into the car to try to stop him driving. We were good mates. But suddenly, nothing. He's moved back up to Birmingham with his parents. I go and see him every time we play up there but always with other United players along. We just can't find anything to say to each other when we're on our own.

SIMMS: Who did you pal up with after Trevor's accident?

GROVES: Nobody really. From then on I became a loner. I was sick to death of the company of most of the other players. I'm not the most popular person at the club you know, Ed. I'm not exactly modest and I speak my mind. It's not won me any friends at United. They think I'm a brash Yankee bastard. The only two players I've really got on with since Trev was put out of the game are Winner Williams and Billy

Willson. Winner is a real solid guy. I wish I had his principles and character. He's the most honest person I've ever met in my life. I not only like him but I also respect him. I can't say that about many people at United. The common bond between Billy Willson and me is, as if you haven't guessed, booze. I really started to hit the bottle after Trev's accident. Some nights I was knocking back a bottle of vodka in one session, usually with Billy along. Sometimes in clubs, sometimes in pubs, but more often than not in my apartment. About six months ago I realized I had to put the brake on my boozing. Screwing wasn't causing me any problems but the drink I was pouring down me began to have an effect. Not so much in my performances on the pitch but in my mind. I was getting so that I couldn't remember what I had done the night before. These blank spots began to frighten me and I started to cut right back on my consumption. Gradually I began to ease my way out of Billy's company. I could see he was becoming a hopeless alcoholic. And I do mean hopeless. If you could see him first thing in the morning you'd get a shock. He has the shakes and has to have a drink to steady himself before joining the team for training. To make matters worse, he is violent to the point of being murderous when he has reached a certain danger point with his drinking. Anyway, no sooner had I given Billy the slip than I was suddenly involved with his wife. She made all the running. Presented herself at my apartment one night and it developed from there. That's another fine mess I've got me into, Stanley.

SIMMS: What finally prompted you to leave your grandparents' place in Southgate?

GROVES: I lived with them for my first two years as a professional but the atmosphere began to get a bit edgy. United supporters found out where I lived and used to come round and make a nuisance of themselves. I didn't mind so much but old Grandpa got real grumpy and sore at them. In his mind, all football fans are hooligans and should be caned on sight.

What finally prompted me to move out was when mom started going out on a regular basis with an old boyfriend of hers. I was delighted for mom but I just somehow couldn't adapt to seeing her with a man other than dad. Sounds crazy I know coming from a ram like me but it got so I wanted to row with mom so that I could tell her what I thought of what she was doing. But good sense got the better of me and rather than cause damage that I could never repair I moved out.

First off, I lived with Trev. And we know how that ended. Then I moved into the apartment I've got now in Kensington. I've got £50,000 invested in that apartment block. It's nice to be able to keep an eye on my investment. I'm the only undesirable resident living there.

SIMMS: Fine, Jackie. That's a good session. I suggest we wind it up here and have another hour or so tomorrow. What are your movements?

GROVES: After training we are all off to a hotel out at Hendon. Staying there for two nights and then going direct to Wembley on Saturday at 1.15. Tell you what, Ed, meet me at the training ground tomorrow at midday and I'll arrange it with Scott Ryder to let you come to the hotel with us for a couple of hours. That's if Billy Willson's not eaten me alive by then ...

Transcript of Tape-recording No. 5 Ends

10

BUBBLES of perspiration were breaking through the powdered make-up on the face of Harvey Rhodes as he read my introduction off the audio-cue that was positioned directly ahead of him alongside camera No. 1.

My segment of his chat show, *Talk to Harvey*, was being pre-recorded and would be tagged on to the end of his 'live' transmission on Friday evening. I had been primed beforehand to imagine that this was Friday, not Wednesday. After three V and Ts in the hospitality room and two before I had left my apartment, I was feeling in a happy, relaxed mood as I watched Harvey on a monitor while I waited for the doors in front of me to slide open at the mention of my name.

'And now to my last guest of the evening,' he said in a plummy voice that carried only a faint suggestion of its Warwickshire origin. 'He is a young man who was born in the United States of America but came home here to England to make his fame and fortune. I say "home to England" because he is following in the footsteps of his father who was one of the greatest of all exponents of our national sport, Association Football. He is carrying on the family traditions of being an outstanding footballer but has gained even more notoriety for his actions off the field of play. Tomorrow on the sacred turf of Wembley, this young man carries the hopes of millions of English football supporters when he plays for United against the New York Comets in the very first Anglo-American Cup Final. Tonight he has come here to talk to Harvey. Would you please welcome the young man who literally has the world at his feet, ladies and gentlemen, Jackie Groves ...'

The audience, responding to a man waving a placard bearing the order 'APPLAUSE', applauded. I watched the monitor as Harvey Rhodes rose from his chair to greet me. The doors remained shut. Suddenly there was a scuffling alongside me and an overalled workman, scrambling on all fours, prised at the crack in the middle of the sliding doors – but they wouldn't budge.

The applause of the audience slowly died away until it almost sounded like a slow handclap. Over the microphone came a comment from Harvey Rhodes that was definitely not on the audio-cue. 'Oh fuck,' he said.

I was whisked back up to the hospitality room while engineers tried to find the fault. Two V and Ts and much laughter later I was guided by my shapely navigator back to the position behind the sliding doors while an even sweatier-looking Harvey Rhodes went through the introduction patter again. '... Ladies and gentlemen, Jackie Groves ...'

Applause. Rhodes arose. The doors stayed shut. This time two studio hands tried to force them open. No joy. Back to the hospitality room. One more V and T. I was now flying high.

After hurried discussions and much cursing between the studio executives, it was decided that Harvey would do the introduction and then the camera would backtrack and pan to reveal me sitting alongside him. Of course, all this talk gave me time for one more V and T. It was a nicely pissed Jackie Groves who waved in acknowledgment as the audience dutifully applauded Harvey's tired-sounding introduction.

I was in that sort of half-drunken state where you know that you are half-drunk but confident you can hide the fact from everybody. What happens, of course, is that you start trying to talk carefully but succeed only in tripping over your tongue and putting in h's where they shouldn't be and all s's become sh's. This was how I performed when I started to talk to Harvey.

'Do you get nervous on the eve of a big match like this, Jackie?' Rhodes asked, wiping the back of his hand over his top lip where a pool of perspiration had gathered.

'Hive never suffered from nervesh,' I said, grinning inanely as Harvey's eyes opened as wide as if matchsticks had suddenly been stuck into them. He was now showered in his own sweat as he looked in terror at his notes to see what he should ask next of the drunken idiot facing him.

'What sort of preparations have you made for tomorrow's match following the marvellous championship-clinching performance against Wanderers on Monday?' he asked, his eyes pleading with me to give an articulate reply.

'We trained exsheptionally hard thish morning,' I said, then suddenly remembering that I was supposed to pretend that this was Friday. 'I mean on Wedneshday morning. Our coach Hugh Blackley shaid he wanted to run all the celebration liquid out of our shytemsh.'

Harvey Rhodes had visibly turned chalk-white under his now soggy make-up. I gave him a wide grin that turned crooked as I tried to pump up his confidence.

'You have a reputation for being – and I quote from your cuttings – "a fun-loving playboy who plays hard on and off the pitch". Would you describe yourself as a playboy?' Harvey looked like a hypnotist as he tried to will me into an intelligent response.

'It'sh a media cliché,' I said, feeling that I was back in Eddie's office. 'They've given me thish image but what is a himage? It's the exclushive property of Fleet Shtreet, Ed . . . I mean, Harv . . .'

The studio floor manager, wearing headphones, waved a large card from under camera No. 1 in the direction of Harvey. It carried the instruction, 'CUT AWAY'. Harvey looked away from me and into camera No. 2 and read from another audio-cue: 'Now to give you a taste of the sort of magic we hope to see from Jackie Groves at Wembley tomorrow, here is a selection of some of his greatest goals.'

He then turned to me and snarled, 'You're pissed, you bastard.'

'Blame your hoshpitality room,' I slurred. 'And your doorsh that never open.'

The floor manager, listening to a voice in his headphones, said: 'You're back on in one minute, Harv. Big Chief upstairs says we must carry on because we shall soon be into overtime for the crews and that would cost the company thousands.'

Poor Harvey, now looking as if somebody had thown a bucket of water over him, leant close to me. 'Pull yourself together, you little cunt,' he said through a smile so that his audience could not interpret his mood. 'There will be twelve million people watching this on Friday. Now for God's sake look lively.'

I sat up straight in my chair as Harvey looked into camera No. 1 and read from the audio-cue. 'They were just six of the marvellous goals Jackie Groves has scored since following in his father's footsteps in the United and England teams,' he said, then turning side on to talk to me: 'Your late father was obviously a great influence on your career, Jackie.'

'Yesh,' I said, striving mightily to sound coherent. 'Dad wash a great influensh on my career. He taught me everything I know and thish ish why I want to play at Wembley on Shaturday. It hash alwaysh been my dream to play at Wembley ever sinch Dad ushed to tell me hall about it when hi wash a little boy in America.'

Harvey decided to battle manfully on. 'You were recently described in a newspaper article as being "SOCCER'S CASANOVA, THE STRIKER WHO ALWAYS SCORES BETWEEN THE GOAL POSTS AND THE BEDPOSTS",' he read from his prepared list of questions. 'Most sportsmen ration their love making before their events. You apparently don't . . .'

'Hi'm writing an autobogphy called "Shoccer Cashanova".' I revealed, remembering Eddie's instruction to try to plug the book. 'I pershonally thrive on making love and never feel it interferesh with my football.'

'Have you ever thought of marrying and settling down?' Harvey asked, hardly bothering to listen to my replies. He just wanted to get the interview over. So did I. I was busting a gut.

'Are you proposhing to me, Harvey?' I asked, a stab at humour that was greeted with gales of laughter from the audience who at last had an excuse to release giggles that had been stifled during fifteen minutes of pure farce.

Harvey laughed nervously. 'Is there any special woman in your life?' he asked.

'Only my mom,' I said. 'I have no plansh to shettle down and marry. Why should hi when hi'm having such a great time?'

'Quite,' said Harvey, almost breathing a sigh of relief as he got a wind-up signal from the floor manager. 'Well, it's certainly been an experience talking to you this evening, Jackie. It only leaves me to wish you, on behalf of all your millions of fans out there, good luck with United against the Comets tomorrow. I'm sure you're going to have a ball.'

The audience-cue man waved his 'APPLAUSE' card and the orchestra played the closing theme music.

I leaned confidentially forward and whispered to Harvey: 'Where's the can?'

There was a roar of laughter from the audience as I slipped out of my chair and on to the floor.

'You realize there's no way we can transmit that, Harv,' the director was saying as I stood swaying at the hospitality bar. 'It would make us the laughing stock of the country.'

'Who let the bastard get pissed out of his skull?' asked Harvey, as if I wasn't there listening.

'It'sh your doorsh fault,' I said. 'If they'd opened I wouldn't have kept coming back up to thish hoshpitality room.'

'The idea of this hospitality room,' Harvey said, continuing to ignore me, 'is to loosen the tongues of our guests, not drown them. Are you sure we can't edit the interview so that we can at least show a few minutes?'

'But the footballer chappie sounds as though he's talking Russian half the time,' said the director. 'If there's sixty seconds of usable film I will be surprised.'

'What's the chance of getting him back on Friday for a live transmission?' the producer asked.

'Minus nil,' said Harvey. 'We had to get on our knees to Scott Ryder to get him here this evening. He won't let him out of his sight on Friday.'

Harvey suddenly spun round and faced me. 'You are a king-size shit, Groves,' he spat. 'Your brains are in your feet.'

'Drop it, Harvey darling,' said the director. 'He's not worth wasting your breath on.'

'I'll shmash your fashe in if you inshult me again,' I growled, my drunkenness suddenly submerged by wild anger. 'You lot got me pisshed.'

The producer waved a uniformed doorman over. 'Take Mr Groves to the canteen and get him several cups of hot black coffee, there's a good man,' he said. 'I'll arrange for a studio car to take him home in an hour's time.'

'Come on Jackie, old son,' said the large Cockney doorman.

'We'll take a nice slow walk to the canteen and I'll tell you how United can win on Saturday.'

As he steered me towards the door, I turned and called to Harvey: 'Give my love to Lizzie.'

That was his breaking point after an evening of high tension. He came charging at me like a mad bull, with his head down. The doorman tried to block him but all three of us fell in a heap on the floor under the power of Harvey's angry rush.

For some stupid reason I started to giggle as Harvey began to pummel me with both fists. His attack lasted only a few seconds before, panting like an exhausted old man, he was pulled off me by the doorman.

'I know all about you and Liz, you shit-faced cretin,' he said between huge gasps for breath. 'You should get your balls cut off. That would stop you fucking everything in sight.'

Now the producer produced. 'That's enough, Harvey,' he said. 'I know all five witnesses who have seen and heard this sorry little episode. If one word gets into the newspapers I will find out who did it and see that he is fired. Now, doorman, can you please get that – that – footballer out of here.'

I was still giggling as the doorman firmly steered me out into the corridor and towards the canteen. 'D'you know shomething,' I confided to my navigator. 'I don't think I'll ever talk to Harvey again.'

Even the doorman had to laugh.

Way off in the distance I could hear bells. What day was it, I wondered. I buried my head deeper into my pillow but the bells wouldn't go away. Slowly it dawned on me that it was the front door bell. Somebody was giving it a hammering. I looked at my watch as I stumbled into my dressing-gown. It was eight-thirty. Presumably on Thursday morning.

The door bell was still ringing. 'I'm coming, for Christ's

sake!' I shouted which brought home the sudden realization that I had an aching head.

I wrenched the door open and looked up into the face of Billy Willson.

Nobody would believe it if I put all this in my book.

11

BILLY WILLSON's entrance was not what I had expected. My fear was that he would smash the door down to get at me but he came in almost sheepishly, hunched over like a man in mourning. He looked as hung over as I felt.

'Sorry it's so early, Jackie,' he mumbled. 'It's just that you and I have got to talk.'

My mind was somersaulting as I led him into the lounge. Surely if he had known about Jen and me he would have knocked the hell out of me by now.

'Coffee?' I said, as he dropped heavily into an armchair. 'You look as if you could do with one. I'll put the kettle on.'

I went into the kitchen and made two cups of instant coffee. Black. While waiting for the kettle to boil, I cleaned my teeth and sluiced my face with cold water. I wanted to have a clear head to hear what Billy had to say.

When I returned to the lounge, Billy was sitting staring vacantly into space as if he was in deep shock. He was startled back into awareness when I handed him his coffee.

'Thanks,' he said. 'I was miles away then. I've been up right through the night. Walked here from our place.'

'Walked?' I said, unable to believe I had heard right. 'But it must be eight miles or more.'

'I'd had a skinful and wanted to walk it out of my system,' he said, unable to hide the tremble in his hands as he drank his coffee. 'Also I wanted to try and get some clear thinking done. You know everybody knows, don't you?'

I was shocked at the casual way he dropped it into the conversation. 'Knows what?' I asked, fearing the reply.

'About you and Jennie, you silly bastard,' he said, not with anger but in a matter-of-fact way. 'The whole bloody world seems to know.'

I searched desperately for something to say. 'We're not seeing each other any more,' was all I could manage.

'I couldn't give a fuck,' he said. 'We're all through anyway. There was a time, Jackie, when I would have broken your back for what you've done.'

Now it was my turn to tremble as I drank my coffee.

'But I've become immune to it,' he continued, repeating I suspected the conversation he had been having with himself during the eight-mile walk. 'If it wasn't you, she'd be at it with somebody else. She's sick, you know.

'In the first year of our marriage I caught her having it off with a copper in Aberdeen. Gave him and her a good thrashing. She pleaded for me to forgive her, so we got back together again. A year later I had to get out of Scottish football because of a scandal involving her and a reserve goalkeeper at our club.'

'Christ, I'm sorry, Billy,' I said, with real sympathy for the big man who had been broken by marriage.

'It's not me who needs your sympathy,' he said. 'It's Jennie. I don't know what's going to become of her. You're about her sixth partner that I know of since I've been at United.'

This statistic startled me. 'Then why haven't you kicked her out before?' I asked, suddenly wondering just what made big Billy Willson tick.

'You wouldn't understand, wee man,' he said. 'Even now I love the lassie. It would be different if we could have bairns. But it's no-go for me. I've been to see top medical specialists but I just can't produce. I'm like a great big empty bloody barrel.'

Again I felt a wave of sympathy for this man of granite, a legendary figure in British football because of his feats of strength on the soccer pitch:

He's six foot five
And just as wide
Here comes Billy Willson
To eat you alive . . .

'I suppose you know that Fleet Street are digging up dirt about Jen and me,' I said, relieved to have the chance to tell him, knowing I was not going to get his 210-lb frame hammering into me in response. He was no lightweight puncher like Harvey Rhodes.

'Aye, I want to talk to you about that,' he said, coming to another rehearsed area of his speech. 'I'm trying to work out a new life, Jackie, and I'm going to need your help.

'What I'm intending to do, although I've signed no papers or anything yet, is sell a story to the *Sunday Herald.* They've told me they will pay me twenty grand for a four-part series.

'Obviously, the first part has got to cover what's been going on behind my back between you and Jennie.'

'They were going to write it anyway,' I said, 'so you might as well make some bread out of it. What does Jennie say?'

'Haven't told her yet,' he replied, standing up and pacing the floor as he outlined his future. 'I shall arrange for her to get half the money. I'm going to ask for thirty grand because in return for their money the *Herald* will get the exclusive news that I am quitting United.'

I felt myself gape. There was nothing I could find to say, so I just let him carry on with his eight-mile talk.

'The first thing I'm going to do as soon as Saturday's Final is over is get myself booked into a private clinic for a long drying-out session. I've made up my mind to beat the booze problem. That's got to be my first step. Then, and this is where you can help, Jackie, I want to get myself fixed up with an American club. I reckon I've got four more years of good football left in me and that's time enough to establish myself in the States where I can build a new future.'

America. I wondered if Billy knew that in this same apartment just a couple of days before his wife had also been talking of a future across the Atlantic. With me. I decided not to mention it. Let sleeping giants lie.

'They will fall over themselves to sign you, Billy,' I said encouragingly and meaning it, because he was still one of the world's most effective central defenders. 'But how about your contract with United?'

'I followed you into the boardroom yesterday for a meeting with the chairman,' he revealed. 'He suggested that a mutual ending of my contract would be the best thing all round. Quite a character, that Turner. He knew I'd been on the piss for the last two years and said the club were getting more than a little tired of bailing me out of trouble. I've run up bills for more than two grand while wrecking places in the last year. The crazy thing is I can't remember any of it.'

'I can't see that you'll be needing my help to get to America then,' I said, 'provided you mean it about kicking the bottle.'

'You can put a good word in for me once you're back over there,' he said. 'This *Herald* story is going to make things look really bad for me. I'm going to admit that I've got a drink problem and once the story is published clubs are going to be frightened to take a chance with me. But once I'm dried out

I'm sure I can start all over again in the States. What d'you think?'

Suddenly I felt only warmth for the man I had been dodging all week. I stood up and shook him by the hand. 'I'll do everything I can to get you over there,' I said. 'That's a promise.'

Billy laughed for the first time since his arrival. 'The last thing I did before leaving the boardroom yesterday was make a promise,' he said. 'The chairman is desperate to win the Final on Saturday. I've promised to do my best. We'll both be playing our last game for United. Let's try and make it a winner.'

Scott Ryder was wearing what we players called his 'television clothes'. The only time he wore a tracksuit at the training ground was when the television cameras were there, and they were out in force for this final session before we moved off to our hotel headquarters out at Hendon.

Billy Willson had been excused training because he had what the Press were told was a heavy cold. He was in fact catching up on his sleep at my apartment and had arranged to meet up with the rest of the team at Hendon after a visit to the *Sunday Herald* offices to sign contracts for his series.

All the major international agencies were represented at an English soccer training ground for what must have been the first time in history. They had been giving massive coverage to the Anglo-American Cup Final and the match was to be screened 'live' on coast-to-coast TV in the States.

After an hour's ball work and light exercises under the supervision of Hugh Blackley, we were given an hour-long tactics talk by Ryder, who upset the NBC camera crew by refusing to let them film it.

The American style of total exposure in sport was completely foreign to Ryder with his head-in-the-sand approach to publicity that continued to anchor the selling of English football to the public. The media were regarded in most quarters as 'a necessary evil' and the wide-spread attitude seemed to be: 'Tell them as little as possible.'

Ryder grudgingly agreed to hold a Press conference after the training session and was relieved when the American Press asked if I could accompany him. He had somebody who would help carry the load.

The *New York Times* representative set the ball rolling with a question that immediately roused Ryder to anger. 'The rumour persists, Mr Ryder, that the Comets are negotiating to buy Jackie Groves,' he said. 'Can you please tell us whether this is in fact so?'

'I am here to answer questions about Saturday's Final,' snapped Ryder, 'not to involve myself with conjecture about rumours.'

'The New York papers are talking about a two million dollar deal,' said the Associated Press reporter.

'I don't give a damn what any papers are saying,' growled Ryder. 'Can you please confine questions to the Final or I am afraid this conference is going to be over before it starts.'

'I'd like to address a question to Jackie,' said the man from Reuters. 'Would you like to play professional soccer in the land of your birth?'

'One day in the future, yes,' I said before Ryder could stop me answering. 'But there's still a lot I want to achieve with United first. I will be happy to give a fuller answer after Saturday's Final which means so much to me.'

'Exactly why does it mean so much, Jackie?' asked the *Daily Mail*, anxious that an English journalist should get a look-in before the American reporters made it a monopoly.

'I suppose it means more to me than most because for a start I am an Anglo-American,' I said, 'and I think that this competition will become equal in importance and prestige to the European Cup. It has already caught the public imagination on both sides of the Atlantic and I am very keen to be on the winning side in the very first Final.

'Secondly, it has a special meaning to me because it is

being played at Wembley. It will be the first time I have ever played there and that will be a dream come true. Ever since I can remember I have wanted to play at Wembley. My father told so many stories about the ground when I was a youngster that the stadium has been elevated to an almost sacred place in my mind. As any of you here who know me will confirm, I am a boring walking record book on Wembley. If you've got a few hours to spare I could tell you about the first ever Final in 1923 when a policeman on a white horse cleared the pitch of spectators so that the match could start. I can tell you about the first time the FA Cup went out of England when Cardiff beat Arsenal at Wembley in 1927. Then there's the Stanley Matthews Final of 1953 when Blackpool came from behind to beat Bolton four-three. Like I was saying, Wembley is a very special place for me.'

'Something you've not mentioned,' said the cynical man from the *Post*, 'is the meaning of money in this match. Doesn't the fact that the sponsors of the Final are putting up a prize of $100,000 to be shared by the winning side help to give it special emphasis?'

'I'm a professional and obviously the money is an atttraction,' I said. 'But I would honestly play for nothing just for the chance of running out on to the Wembley pitch. I know it sounds corny but it's true.'

'Can you give us your line-up yet, Scott?' asked the man from the *Evening News* who had a pressing edition time. The daily paper boys had been hoping to avoid that question until it was too late to make the evenings.

'It depends on a fitness test tomorrow morning on Theo Hall,' said Ryder, now talking in a relaxed fashion because he was in territory where he felt comfortable. He could talk about his team for hours on end without tiring. 'Theo got a knock against Wanderers on Monday. He's still having treatment and I shall see how he goes with a ball at his feet tomorrow before making any definite decision.'

'What if he fails the fitness test?' asked the *Express*.

'That's something I want to sleep on,' said Ryder, cannily playing his cards close to his chest because he wanted the Comets to think he had an alternative that they didn't know about. He wasn't fooling the Press boys, though.

'It would surely mean Frank MacLaren coming into the attack as he did on Monday,' the *Mirror* man said, framing his question as a statement of fact.

'You will have to wait and see, gentlemen,' said Ryder. 'I shall name the team when I am ready and not before.'

'What about Billy Willson?' asked the *Sun*.

'What about him?' Ryder snapped, over-reacting to a perfectly innocent inquiry. The more observant journalists would now be suspecting that the 'cold' was an excuse rather than a reason for his absence. But they would have to wait for the *Sunday Herald* before they could fully fathom the edginess in Ryder's voice.

'I was just wondering how bad his cold is?' added the reporter from the *Sun*, his mind making a mental note to take a careful look at the Willson situation.

'It's not serious,' said Ryder, relieved that he was not being asked more probing questions about the club captain. 'He will be joining us at our Hendon hotel later in the day.'

I excused myself from the conference, leaving the posse of journalists chipping away at Ryder for quotes like quarry workers. Eddie Simms peeled off from the back and joined me as I walked back to the locker-room to shower and change for the bus ride to Hendon.

'Is it okay for me to join you at Hendon for a taping session?' he asked.

'I've cleared it with Ryder,' I said, 'but he doesn't want you coming in the bus. He says if he lets one journalist on everybody is going to want to climb aboard.'

'That's a fair point,' said fair-minded Eddie. 'I'll follow you over in my car and you can give me an hour of your time whenever it suits you.'

All the other players had left the locker-room when I came out of the shower. I dried myself and dressed in two minutes flat. Something that my years in professional football had taught me was how to become a quick-change artist.

I opened my locker and took out the boots that I would be wearing at Wembley. Jammed into the right boot was an envelope with my name scrawled on the outside in capital letters.

After packing the boots in my hold-all, I tore open the envelope and read the brief note:

> You're going to get your kneecaps blown
> off at Wembley.
> An ex-fan

It was funny that I should have thought of my book at a moment like this. No publisher would ever believe it, I said to myself.

I had received threats before but this one somehow *felt* different. It had scared the shit out of me.

12

'YOU'VE *got* to tell somebody,' advised Eddie Simms as he read the note in my hotel room at Hendon. 'Obviously it could be a hoax. Some sick person's idea of a joke. But just suppose it's a genuine threat? Let's be honest, Jackie, there are a few people around who would like to blow your kneecaps off.'

There was a moment's silence as I paraded a procession of suspects on my memory screen. It was a long queue.

'You're the only person I've shown the note,' I said, taking the piece of plain white paper back from him and replacing it in the envelope. 'I've got a gut feeling that whoever wrote it means what he says.'

'Or *she* means what *she* says,' added Eddie, a thought that had already crossed my mind a few hundred times.

'I think I should confide in somebody,' I agreed with Ed. 'But who? If I were to show this to Scott Ryder he would drop me from the team like a hot brick. I'm determined to play at Wembley on Saturday and I'm not going to let some nut stop me.'

'What about John Turner?' Eddie suggested. 'From the tone of the conversation you had with him in the boardroom yesterday, he sounds as if he would give you the sort of advice you need.'

'That's a good i-dea, Stanley,' I said in my best Oliver Hardy voice. 'Trouble is, how do I get to see him? We're confined to barracks here. The only time we're going out is *en masse* this evening when Ryder is taking us to the cinema.'

Sherlock Simms took charge. He fished his directory of contacts out of his briefcase and telephoned Turner's City office.

'When he comes to the 'phone,' said Eddie, 'tell him you need to see him urgently and that it needs to be away from here. Suggest that he tells Ryder that he wants to talk to you about something to do with the move to America. You never know, Jackie, it just might be Ryder who is making the threat.'

Neither of us even raised a smile.

Twenty minutes later Ryder came to my room. 'The chairman is sending his car here for you,' he said. 'He wants to talk to you about next Monday's Press conference and the Comets announcement. I've told him I want you back here by six-thirty to join us for our visit to the pictures.'

Turner's chauffeur-driven Rolls whisked me around the back doubles of North London and into the City in under twenty minutes, despite heavy traffic that was as ever blocking the North Circular Road. The chairman had an impressive oak-panelled penthouse suite of offices in a new skyscraper that towered over Mansion House and the Corn Exchange.

His pride in United was evident in the outer office where the walls were hung with a dozen pictures of big-match moments and team photographs in which he was always prominent. I was ushered into the inner room by his secretary, a middle-aged woman of great elegance who was clearly employed for her efficiency rather than her bedworthiness.

Turner sat behind a leather-topped desk big enough to cater for the needs of half a dozen office workers. 'Thank you, Miss Wolfe,' he said. 'Can you please intercept all calls for the next twenty minutes and only put through those that are absolutely vital.'

He came from behind his desk and shook me warmly by the hand. 'I didn't expect to have the pleasure of your company again so soon, lad,' he said, steering me across the room to a large picture window. 'While you're here, take a look at the best view of London that you can get. On a clear day, you can even see Wembley Stadium from here. Reet grand, don't you think?'

It certainly was. You could see the Thames snaking away east past the Tower of London and through the East End docklands with their redundant cranes looking like abandoned oil derricks. Off to the west, you could follow the river along the Embankment with its criss-cross of bridges, past the Houses of Parliament and Westminster Abbey and on to Hammersmith and out as far as Chiswick and Windsor.

'From up here it looks the most beautiful city in the world,' I said.

'It *is* the most beautiful city in the world, lad,' said Turner, then chuckling as he added: 'Particularly when you own a great heap of it. Of course, you can get much higher than this over in New York. But just remember, Jackie, the higher you go the farther there is to fall.'

The tour of inspection and the philosophy lesson over, he gestured for me to sit in a leather armchair that he moved to the centre of the room. He then returned to his seat, lit a cigar and officially opened our meeting.

'Right, lad, spit it out,' he said by way of invitation. 'What's the problem?'

I explained how I had found the note stuffed into my boot

after training and handed him the envelope. He read the letter, folded it and replaced it in the envelope.

'You were right to show me this, Jackie,' he said after a moment's thoughtful gaze in the direction of the picture window. 'There are so many bloody maniacs around these days. You can't be too careful.'

'I don't want it to make me miss the match,' I said, unable to keep a pleading tone out of my voice.

'Too bloody right,' agreed Turner, picking up the envelope and fanning at the end of his Havana to send cigar smoke spiralling up to the ceiling. 'This just might be somebody's idea of a joke. But we can't take chances. I don't think you're in any immediate danger because t'note specifically mentions Wembley. Let me have a quiet word with a contact of mine at New Scotland Yard. On the hush hush, of course. He'll advise me as to what's best. Meantime, lad, it might help if you start working out who you think might be responsible for this. Surely nobody at t'club would sink to this level?'

So far, I had got my short list down to about one thousand suspects.

Turner's chauffeur had me back at the hotel within an hour of leaving. Eddie Simms was still there, sitting in the corner of the lounge reading in the evening paper how Scott Ryder was delaying selection of his team until a fitness test on Theo Hall. All the players were having an afternoon rest in their rooms until dinner at 5.45. There was over an hour to go, so I invited Eddie back up to my room for our delayed taping session.

Transcript of Tape-recording No. 6

SIMMS: I think it will do you good, Jackie, to talk for a while about something other than that bastard note. That's why I waited around in case you came back. You need to get it out of your mind otherwise it could drive you around the twist trying to think who left it in your locker.

GROVES: You're right as usual, Ed. I've had people threatening me before. But they've always been cranks. I must have had a dozen telephone calls and unsigned letters from people saying they were going to make a mess of me after that car crash with Trev. And I've had a few aggrieved husbands and boyfriends threatening me in my time, usually after their wives or girls have made advances to me, I might add! But there's something different about this one. Something sinister. Like you say, I could go nuts trying to think who could have written it. So let's get off the subject. What do you want to know for the book?

SIMMS: I shall be making Saturday's Final the climax of the book and I need some inside information from you on the build-up to the game. For instance, how much time are you and your team-mates giving to cashing in on the Final? What are you earning from peripheral activities?

GROVES: As you know, we've got a players' perks pool. It's being run for us by Ken Ryan, the club commercial manager. There are twenty shares in the pool. Each of the fourteen players in the first-team squad has a full share. Scott Ryder, Hugh Blackley, Dusty Rhodes and Ken Ryan have a half share each and the remaining four shares will go to the reserve squad.

SIMMS: What is each individual likely to make?

GROVES: Ouch. That will take some working out. For a start, we are hoping to have the $100,000 that the sponsors are offering to the winning team. But even without that we should all be on a great bonus. Admus, the boot manufacturers, are paying a lump sum of £25,000 for us all to wear their boots. I thought I was going to have trouble with Kingfitters, whose boots I wear all season, but my lawyer has told me my contract with them is for League, European and FA Cup games only. Not for the book, Ed, but just between you and me, I shall be wearing my usual boots but with an Admus trademark painted on the side. Several of the other players are doing the same. This is too important a game in which to break in new boots.

SIMMS: Careful with that one. I remember some Cup Finalists doing that a few years back. It rained during the Final and the temporary trademarks washed off. The boot manufacturers threatened to take the players to court until they paid back the advance they had received.

GROVES: Let's just hope it doesn't rain. Perhaps I should take a pot of paint and a brush on the pitch with me!

SIMMS: What about the firm supplying your shirts and shorts?

GROVES: Their deal is with the club. They have a four-year contract with United for £100,000. But they have agreed to chip an extra £12,000 into our pool.

SIMMS: Newspapers, magazines and television?

GROVES: This caused a lot of aggro. There were just six of us wanted for major series by the newspapers: Billy Willson, Paulo Valloso, Mickey Dixon, Theo Hall, Paddy O'Brien and me. We were receiving varying amounts from £2,000 up to £8,000. It all came to about £25,000, plus £200 from each of the newspapers and magazines for our co-operation at picture sessions. A couple of the sports editors refused to chip in any money at all and argued that we got enough free publicity all season. The big trouble was caused by Mickey Dixon. He received £5,000 for a two-part series on his ghosted thoughts about the Final and wanted to keep it for himself. His point was that why should he put £5,000 into the pool while players like Winner Williams and Leftie Wright were not contributing anything. We couldn't get it into his thick skull that we had got into this Final as a team, not as twelve individuals, and that he couldn't have scored his goals without the help of team-mates. In the end we had to compromise. The so-called 'star' players were told they could keep half their earnings from newspaper articles and put half into the pool. I've arranged to have my half, £4,000, sent to Trev up in Birmingham. And I don't want that in the book.

SIMMS: What are you getting from the TV boys?

GROVES: Both companies have paid in £2,000 'disturbance' money and there's an extra £5,000 coming from ITV so that they can have a camera crew with us in the hotel on Saturday morning and on the bus going to Wembley. NBC are paying £3,000 for a 'meet the players' session in front of their cameras immediately after training tomorrow morning.

SIMMS: What about sponsorships and endorsements other than for what you are wearing on the pitch?

GROVES: We are getting £5,000 from Halliwells, the tailors, for wearing their made-to-measure club suits on Saturday. In return they're using blow-up pictures of the team in their suits in their chain of shops and in newspaper advertisements. We'll be getting £1,000 for making sure we are pictured drinking pints of milk at the end of the game and £15,000 for that terrible television commercial we've made where we are singing the praises of that horrible new breakfast cereal, Poppers.

SIMMS: Talking of terrible singing, what do you all stand to make from that record 'United, United'?

GROVES: You mean apart from the prize for Crappiest Record of the Year? The record company paid us £3,000 and we are on a ten per cent royalty, which should be at least two pounds!

SIMMS: Any other major income for the pool? What for instance about the souvenir brochure I saw being hawked outside the ground on Monday night?

GROVES: That's already pulled in £10,000 in advertising revenue and the printing costs should be more than covered by its sale. We've had 40,000 printed and they are selling fast at 50p a time. Last week we spent three hours signing five hundred balls that we have sold to pubs and clubs at £50 a time. They will more than get their money back by raffling them or giving them away as prizes. We all got writers' cramp but it was worth it for the £25,000 the pool will make. Again not for the book, but the reserves helped out with the autographs. There were twenty-two players signing fourteen names!

SIMMS: Anything else you can think of?

GROVES: We got £2,000 from the Exclusive International Sports Club for being guests of honour at their Dinner last week. You see this watch? It's a Final Timekeeper. You'll find all the guys are wearing one. We get the watch free and £10,000 in the pool.

SIMMS: So if you win on Saturday, the pool should net around £200,000 which works out at £10,000 a man plus your club contract that guarantees you what sort of bonus?

GROVES: If we win on Saturday, we each get £7,500. If we lose we pick up £5,000 each.

SIMMS: So it's possible that you could all be richer by £17,500 for this one match. I suppose you realize there are plenty of people in this country who take three years to earn that sort of money. There will be accusations flying of galloping greed among United footballers.

GROVES: You might point out in our defence that this sort of opportunity may come along only once in a footballer's career and that he is entitled to get as much out of it as he can. There will be 100,000 people at Wembley on Saturday and another 400 million or more watching the match live on television around the world. If each of those people paid the twenty-four players at Wembley just 1p for the privilege of watching them, the gross income would be something in excess of £4 million. My maths isn't that great, Ed, but I do know with that sort of loot coming in each player would pick up more than £160,000. You might also point out in the book that a player's career at peak earning power lasts no more than ten years.

SIMMS: I'll get the violin out in a minute, Jackie. You're breaking my heart.

GROVES: It's the footballers from my dad's era I feel sorry for. They were really exploited. Dad used to regularly play in front of crowds of more than 50,000 in First Division matches and his weekly take-home pay was £17, plus a £2 win bonus. You want to listen to Dusty Rhodes on the subject of slave soccer. He really will break your heart. As he told me the other day when he was giving me a massage, the £10,000 bonus we collected for winning the League championship on Monday was as much as he and my dad earned throughout their entire career.

SIMMS: I agree they were under-paid but everything is relative. In the 1940s and 1950s you could stand on the terraces for the equivalent of 10p. Now it costs £1.50 to stand and anything up to £10 to sit. The cheapest seat at Wembley on Saturday is £7.50. Anyway, I want to tackle you on one more perk that you haven't mentioned before we finish this taping session. What about Cup Final tickets? How many do you get from the club and what happens to them?

GROVES: Officially, we are not allowed to have more than thirty tickets each but we have been given an allocation to the pool of a further five hundred tickets. After looking after friends and relatives, we were left with about four hundred. The Power Oil Company bought a hundred off us at £50 a ticket. They distribute them to staff as perks. Ticket tout Harry the Hawk has paid us £12,000 for the other three hundred and expects to get £100 a ticket for them on the black market.

SIMMS: So that's another £17,000 for the pool. The loyal fans who can't get a sniff of a ticket will love you for that.

GROVES: We've got to duck round this one in the book, Eddie. I know I've been saying 'I want to tell it as it really is' in my book but I don't want to shit on the other guys in the club. I would be getting the players I leave behind into tax trouble if I divulged this ticket dodge. Obviously we don't declare the ticket income. Let's face it, the Inland Revenue will be grabbing at least two-thirds of our pool money.

SIMMS: I thought Maggie Thatcher's lot had taken some of the pressure off you big earners.

GROVES: Dropping the top tax bracket to sixty per cent has helped. Before that, we were getting murdered by the taxman. I was going to send *him* a threatening note.

SIMMS: So why do you still have to fiddle Cup tickets?

GROVES: Life for a footballer is short, Ed. You know that. We still have to pay a great whack in tax, so anything we can get away with helps. Our big money earning peak lasts little more than ten years. We'd be fools not to cash in while we can.

SIMMS: That seems a good place to finish this tape, thanks Jackie. I'm sure the man in the street will be interested to know how the players' pool operates and the sort of money that can be earned by reaching a Final.

GROVES: Just go easy on the ticket theme, Ed. Otherwise I'll be getting a lot more threats. From my team-mates.

SIMMS: Don't worry. You'll be able to blue pencil anything you don't like out of the book before it gets to the publishers.

GROVES: I'll hold you to that. We've got it down on record. While I think of it, at our next taping session remind me to tell you about an unbelievable interview I had with Harvey Rhodes on Wednesday. It will make a hilarious chapter for the book ...

Transcript of Tape-recording No. 6 Ends

Winner Williams wondered why I was so quiet and lost in thought on the bus ride to the movie house in Leicester Square. I told him I was thinking ahead to the Final, while in truth I was holding an imaginary identity parade of suspects who might have left that threatening note in my locker.

The movie failed to hold my attention. Up on the screen, Clint Eastwood was shooting holes in a gang of five men who had been hunting him across the great plains of America which as any film buff knew were really the agricultural lands of Italy.

I was trying hard to concentrate on the Spaghetti Western but every shot made my mind switch back to the threatening note.

What, I wondered, must it be like to be shot in the knee-caps?

13

DETECTIVE-SERGEANT COATES, of New Scotland Yard, was sprawled out on my bed as if he had found his last resting place. He had kicked off his brown suède shoes and was lying back staring at the ceiling for inspiration as he questioned me about the threatening note.

I was sitting in an armchair at the side of the bed trying very hard to help him with his detection work but finding it difficult to believe that this pugnacious, rough-hewn Cockney from Bethnal Green was really a crack member of one of Britain's top special crime squads.

I had even less faith in his side-kick, Detective-Constable Roberts, a Welshman who had already virtually blown his cover as a documentary journalist by asking his countryman and idol Winner Williams for an autograph.

Roberts was sitting on the window ledge of my hotel room taking copious notes as Coates quizzed me. John Turner had introduced me to them at training that morning. 'These two gentlemen have been assigned to look after you for the next forty-eight hours,' he said. 'They are tops at their job, so just do as they tell you. I have explained to Scott Ryder exactly who they are and why they are here. He will go along with t'cover story that they're journalists preparing a documentary on you.'

They had now been trailing me for six hours but this was the first opportunity we'd had for a private talk. I kept feeling I had stumbled on to the film set of a whodunnit as Coates conducted his inquiries while chain smoking vile-smelling French cigarettes.

'It would help us enormously, Jackie, me old son, if as your minders we had a rough idea who we're protecting you from,' said Coates in an accent as lazily Cockney as a peal of Bow Bells. 'Do you think you could narrow the field down a bit for us, like. The person most likely to. Know what I mean?'

He turned his head on the pillow and smiled at me, inviting a response. 'Where do I start?' I said, with a shrug of my shoulders. 'I've been drawing up short lists ever since I got the note but the longer I have to think about it the longer the list gets. For all I know, it could be a moron from the terraces because I was outspoken about the United hooligan element in a newspaper interview last week. Described them as mindless thugs.'

'Right an' all,' agreed Coates. 'But that note ain't from a terrace hooligan. The sentiment goes along with their sort of thinking. The thought of shooting somebody's kneecaps would appeal to them. But to put it in writing? Nope. It's too sophisticated for them. I think you've got to come much nearer 'ome, me son.'

'Nearer home?' I queried. 'You mean think of somebody inside the club?'

'Inside or very close to it,' said Coates. 'After all, 'ow many people have access to your dressing-room at the training ground? I had a butchers at it this morning. It would be easy for anybody to slip in and out while you're all training but 'ow would he know which locker is yours?'

'Or she,' interrupted Detective-Constable Roberts, looking up from his notebook.

It prompted Coates to sit up on the bed. 'Why don't you keep your big north and south shut, Dai bach,' he said with heavy sarcasm. 'I would rather Jackie here came up with that sort of thought without prompting from Cardiff's answer to bloody Theo Kojak.'

'There are a few women who'd like to see me shot,' I admitted. 'But I think they would aim at my cock rather than my kneecaps.'

Coates laughed so much at that he nearly rolled off the bed. 'That's lovely, that is Jackie,' he said, still giggling. 'I've read all about you and the birds. Good luck to you, mate. Wish I could get some on the side.'

He suddenly became serious. 'As it 'appens, I think you're right in your assumption that this note ain't from a bird,' he said, taking the letter from the envelope that he had tucked away in an inside pocket of his jacket. 'The sort of birds you go out with wouldn't talk about shooting kneecaps. That's villain's talk, that is. I've seen a few kneecap jobs. Very nasty.'

Sensing that I had tensed at the prospect, Coates quickly added: 'But we ain't going to let nobody ruin a great footballer like Jackie Groves by shooting 'im in the kneecaps are we, Dai?'

'S'right, Sarge,' agreed Roberts, who rationed his words as if they were too precious to give away too many at a time.

A sickening thought struck me. Supposing somebody had decided they were going to take a shot at me from long range during the game? In all my imaginations about having my kneecaps shot, I had conjured up pictures of it happening at close range. I composed myself before making a casual enquiry.

'I have every faith in you two guys to do all you can to protect me at Wembley tomorrow, but what if somebody's going to try to shoot me from up in the stands during the match?' I asked, struggling to keep my composure at the prospect of a lump of red-hot lead smashing into my kneecap at God knows what speed.

'We have gone into that little matter, me old son,' said Coates, using the half-inch stub of one cigarette to light his next one. 'It just so 'appens that Wembley security guards are checking on everybody who goes into the ground tomorrow. But don't feel too flattered. It was planned anyway because of the latest spate of bombings by those terrorist nutcases. So as well as looking for bombs they'll be instructed to sniff around for shooters, 'an all. Ain't you a lucky bloke?'

Coates rested his head back on the pillow and practised blowing smoke rings at the ceiling. I read danger signals of a difficult question coming my way. ''Ow d'you get on with your team-mates, Jackie?' he asked. 'That Paddy O'Brien, f'instance. Would he like to do you any damage?'

'Paddy? He wouldn't hurt a fly,' I said. 'The only time in life that he ever shows aggression is when he's coming off his goal-line to collect the ball. It would be ridiculous to suspect him.'

'Fine,' said Coates. 'There are eleven more players to go, including the substitute. Once we've eliminated all them we can start putting together a short list. Would y'mind giving me your personal assessment of each of the players. Not what they're like as footballers but as people. How y'get on with each of them, like.'

'But it's too ridiculous for words to think that any of my team-mates would want to make such a stupid threat,' I protested. Coates sat up and dangled his legs over the side of the bed. 'Far more unbelievable things have 'appened,' he said. 'People with unbalanced minds do very weird things, y'know.'

'An entire rugby team went down with poisoning in

Merthyr once,' said Detective-Constable Roberts, making for him what amounted to a speech. 'It transpired that a player who had been dropped poisoned their pre-match meal.'

'Thank you, Taff,' said Coates, with a cutting edge to his voice. 'You'd better test United's food before the game tomorrow. Now d'you mind just concentrating on taking notes while Jackie here gives us a run-down on his team-mates.'

'Well I'm not the most popular guy in the locker-room,' I conceded, accepting that it was in my own interests that I should consider each of my team-mates in turn. 'Ronnie Dicks would certainly not vote me his favourite footballer of the century. In fact, he hates my guts. And the feeling is pretty mutual.'

''As he ever threatened you?' asked Coates, his copper's instincts aroused.

'We had a fight once,' I replied. 'In a disco. It was over a girlfriend of his who decided half-way through the evening that she fancied me more than him. We were pulled apart before more than a couple of punches were swapped. Just as well, because I'm a devout coward when it comes to fighting and he used to be an amateur boxing champion. We've hardly exchanged a civilized word since.'

'How long ago was it?' inquired Coates.

'Two, going on three years,' I said.

'Plonk him down on the short list, Dai,' he instructed Roberts. 'But 'e can't be the favourite. If he'd been so keen to do you an injury, 'e would have done it yonks ago. Who's next?'

'Roger Hart,' I said. 'He's like a puppet on strings for Ronnie Dicks. They are inseparable and Hart does whatever Dicks suggests. But he wouldn't have got himself involved in this threatening business. He's the sort of guy who would shoot you on the spot without the warning note. I don't think he's ever planned anything in his life. Come to think of it, the note couldn't have come from him. He can't even write.'

'You are joking, I presume?' Coates asked, chuckling.

'Just about,' I said. 'But I feel sure the note didn't come from him. If it did, he would have meant it as a sick joke and I would have no worries tomorrow.'

'How about Winner Williams?' asked Coates, throwing a glance in the direction of Roberts. 'You can never trust these Welsh buggers, y'know.'

'Do me a favour, Sarge,' Roberts protested before I could get a word in. 'Winner is a Baptist lay preacher. Read the epilogue on telly a couple of Sundays ago, he did . . .'

Coates raised his hands towards the ceiling in a gesture of despair. 'For gawd's sake behave yourself, Taff,' he said, 'otherwise I'll get you transferred back to traffic control. I'm 'ere to interview Jackie Groves not Taffy bleedin' Roberts from the bloody Rhondda.'

I was getting used to the exchanges between Coates and Roberts and was beginning to enjoy them. They were like a double act, with Roberts playing the straight man. And I was beginning to realize that the line of questioning by Coates was shrewd and perceptive; behind the casual front lurked a cunning mind.

'Winner is my closest friend,' I said. 'I would trust him with my life. He's the most honest and sensible person I know.'

Roberts visibly grew several inches taller than his already towering 6 ft 3 ins frame.

'I think we should have a quick chorus of "Land Of Our bleedin' Fathers",' Coates said with good humour rather than malice. I sensed he was studying me closely as he added: 'Now what about Billy Willson?'

'I suppose until yesterday Billy would have been the person most likely to,' I said.

'Meaning he had a strong motive,' Coates said, not questioning but interpreting.

I nodded. 'You'll be able to read all about it in the *Sunday Herald* this weekend,' I said. 'I had formed what you might call an intimate relationship with Jennie Willson, Billy's wife. I thought he would break me in two when he found out, but it turns out I was one of a queue of guys she had been entertaining.'

'And what 'appened yesterday?' asked Coates, adding the third cigarette to his chain since he had been in my room.

'Billy told me their marriage is over,' I said. 'I suppose you know he's got a drink problem?'

'I know more than you think I know, Jackie my son,' Coates said with a smug smile. 'F'instance, I knew about you and Mrs Willson but I wanted you to tell me. And as for Billy and his drinking, I 'appen to know he's been nicked twice for being pissed out of his head in the last three months. But lucky old Billy's 'ad strings pulled for him in 'igh places. Now what makes you so sure 'e won't take some awful revenge on you for knocking off his missus?'

'We talked it out yesterday morning,' I explained. 'He wants me to help get him fixed up with a club in the States.'

'With Alcoholics Anonymous United?' Coates said, laughing at what I considered a joke in poor taste.

'Billy is going to try to dry out this summer,' I said. 'He's a real Jekyll and Hyde guy. One minute he can be as nice as pie and the next ready to fight the world. But I'm sure the note didn't come from him and, anyway, he didn't go to the training ground on Thursday.'

'The note could have been put in your locker any time after you left the training ground on Wednesday,' reasoned Coates. 'Taffy, my old son, put Billy Willson's name down on the short list. He's certainly got a motive. I'll tell you this, Jackie, if I caught you screwing my missus I'd shoot you in the kneecaps. Have you been seeing to any other players' wives or girlfriends?'

'Don't fancy any of them,' I said, having a stab at Coates-style humour which he appreciated. 'Seriously though, I get on reasonably well with most of the other players in the team. Mickey Dixon doesn't like me because I score more goals and pull more girls than he does but that's hardly a motive for wanting to shoot me. Monty Masters is not all that keen on me because I think there's more to life than just football. But he is too loyal to United to want to in any way injure one of the club's players.'

'What about an ex-United player though?' Coates asked, clearly sharing the secret that I was on my way back to the United States. 'Would Monty Masters perhaps be unbalanced enough to want to shoot a player who leaves his beloved United?'

It sounded a daft theory at first but then I recalled the way Monty had reacted when I had nipped off on one of my unscheduled mid-season jaunts. 'He suggested once that I should piss off back to the States because he reckoned I was a disgrace to football,' I told my inquisitor, who considered that reason enough to add his name to the short list of suspects.

We quickly cleared Theo Hall, Paulo Valloso and Leftie Wright of any suspicion, put a question mark over Frank MacLaren because he reckoned he should have my place in the team, and decided that no other player in the club had a motive to threaten my career in football.

'Now what about the officials?' asked Coates, now on his fifth cigarette and looking as if he should carry a Government health warning. 'By all accounts you don't hit it off with Scott Ryder.'

'Scott detests everything I stand for off the pitch,' I admitted. 'He's a religious man who sees me as a sinner beyond salvation.'

'When I was on the beat down in Cardiff,' said Roberts, 'there was a religious nut who went round shooting newsagents just because they sold girlie magazines.'

''Ere we go,' said Coates, feeding off his straight man. 'All Our bleedin' Yesterdays with Taffy Roberts. I can't wait to read your memoirs, Taff.'

I interrupted the banter. 'Look, you can't seriously believe that Scott Ryder would do something as crazy as threaten one of his players a couple of days before the most important match in his managerial career,' I said.

Coates got off the bed and walked around the room, arching his back and yawning like somebody getting up first thing in the morning. 'Just suppose this is a genuine threat and not a hoax,' he said as he stifled a second yawn. 'It's got to have been written by a nut, right? Well from what I can gather, Scott Ryder's not been acting particularly sane lately. I've been told his nerve has gone and that 'e is drinking whisky in his office like water from the tap. I agree it's unlikely that he's the nutter who's threatening you but we've got to put 'im down as an outsider. Like I said to you earlier, people with unbalanced minds do very weird things.'

My mind back-tracked to the scene in the car park at United's ground when I was summoned to see the chairman after training on Wednesday. Ryder's behaviour pattern then could certainly have been classed as unbalanced.

Coates had finished his circuit of the room and was now back on the bed and for the first time since he had joined me after lunch there was not a cigarette burning in his hand or dangling from his mouth. 'How about you and Hugh Blackley?' he asked, again with a knowing look. 'I 'ear you're not exactly bosom pals.'

'Too right,' I admitted. 'He detests me because I refuse to conform to his blinkered tactical ideas. But it's hardly likely that he would do a stupid thing like put a threatening note in my locker. He's not my favourite guy but there's no way you could describe him as unbalanced. Blackley knows exactly what he wants and that's to be manager of United. The only person he'd like to see shot is Scott Ryder.'

That brought a chuckle from Coates and then he gave further evidence of how much homework he had done by tossing in another suspect. 'Tell me about your assessment of the directors,' he said, 'and in particular George Stoughton.'

'John Turner *is* the United board of directors,' I said. 'There are five directors with him but they have about as much say in the running of the club as the tea ladies. I've had no dealings at all with any of the board apart from Turner and George Stoughton. I used to be a regular house guest of the Stoughtons. He was always throwing parties and liked to have the players along to show off like trophies. I've never particularly liked the man. He's too full of his own self importance.'

'But you did like Mrs Stoughton?' Coates said, encouraging me to tell him what he obviously already knew.

'We had an association that lasted about a year,' I said. 'I finished it about six months ago. She started to take it too seriously and so I stopped seeing her.'

'Was she bitter when you packed her in?' asked Coates. 'Bitter enough to have wanted you shot in the kneecaps?'

'I thought we decided that was villain's talk,' I said. 'If you're going to start putting women on the short list we could be here all night.'

'It all depends on what sort of woman Mrs Stoughton is,' said Coates. 'Would you say she was unbalanced?'

'Pam Stoughton, as I'm sure you have already discovered, is a beautiful woman who used to be a top fashion model until she became George Stoughton's second wife,' I said, filling in details that Coates doubtless knew before starting this interrogation. 'She is thirty years younger than her husband and still married to him only because his money provides her with all the materialistic things she wants from life. She goes outside her marriage for her physical comforts. When I told her I wouldn't be seeing her any more, she had a short, hysterical outburst. Crying. Asking me to marry her. That sort of rubbish. At that time, she would have been quite capable of shooting me. Right in the balls. But it was six months ago and I have not seen her since.'

'Did George Stoughton ever find out about the affair?' Coates asked, lighting the inevitable cigarette.

'Not that I know of,' I said. 'I see him most match days and I have not sensed any change in our relationship. I don't go to his parties any more but I think that's mainly because John Turner ordered him to stop inviting the players because he felt it was bad for the image of the club. There is always a lot of drink flowing at any party given by the Stoughtons.'

Coates seemed satisfied that we had covered the area that mattered, although I still found it hard to believe that anybody connected with United would make such a stupid yet chilling threat against me. When I thought back to how the fan at Birmingham had spat at me on Saturday and with such a look of deep hatred on his face, I realized that I could have filled the London telephone directory with a list of suspects.

We had talked our way round to teatime, and Coates and Roberts were to join me at the table. Before leaving the hotel room, I opened the window wide to try to clear the air of the stench of French cigarettes.

The one thing bugging me was what Coates said about the training ground. Anybody could get into the locker-room but how would they know which locker was mine unless they were connected with the club? There were no numbers or names on the lockers, so how had they known in which locker to leave the envelope?

We got the answer to that puzzle as we were about to attack our second round of toast. Dusty Rhodes came strolling past our table on his bowed old pro's legs when he suddenly stopped and asked: 'Did you get that envelope I left in your locker yesterday, Jackie? One of the secretaries found it in the letter box at the ground so I brought it out to training in case it was important.'

Detective-Sergeant Coates looked as if he was about to suffer a severe bout of indigestion. 'Excuse me,' he said. 'I'm just going to nip outside for a quick smoke.'

We all went to our rooms at ten with orders to go straight to bed. Hugh Blackley always did a round of the rooms when we stayed at hotels to make sure we *were* in bed. Alone.

Over the years, he and Scott Ryder had reluctantly

accepted the fact that I was an incurable insomniac and this was why I had a hotel room to myself while other players shared. But this didn't stop Blackley checking that I was in my room if not my bed. And he was always careful to look out for any tell-tale signs of hidden female company. I had smuggled girls into my wardrobe and even under my bed before now but on this night when Blackley made his call I was alone – with my thoughts.

'Hope you get a good night's sleep, Jackie,' he said, obviously meaning it. 'We want you wide awake on that Wembley pitch tomorrow. You're the man who can win it for us. Sweet dreams.'

As Blackley closed the door I made a mental note to strike him off the list of suspects.

I turned the television on and watched it from my bed. How, I wondered, were they going to get round my absence from the *Talk to Harvey* show.

Harvey, sweating profusely, apologized that they could not show my recorded interview for 'technical reasons'. In my place they had Harvey talking to the Comets' centre-forward Wilhelm van der Veer, the Dutch international who had been signed for Real Madrid for one million dollars eighteen months ago.

It had been arranged at such short notice that Harvey clearly had not had time to swot up on his subject. He asked a string of cliché questions and got a string of cliché answers in an interview that was so flat and lifeless that it almost cured my insomnia.

But just as I was drifting off to sleep I was startled awake by a knocking on the door. It was Scott Ryder.

'I won't keep you long, Jackie,' he said, his breath smelling strongly of Scotch. 'Just wanted to tell you how sorry I am to hear about that stupid threat you've received. I sometimes wonder what this world is coming to.'

He dropped himself heavily into my armchair as if he had come for a lengthy stay, so I made myself comfortable by sitting on the edge of my bed and leaning back with my elbows on the pillow.

'The chairman doesn't want me to do this but I feel I must give you the option of pulling out of the game,' he said. 'We could say you pulled a muscle in training.'

'I appreciate your concern for my safety,' I said, with genuine warmth. 'But to be honest, that's the last thing I want to do. This game means more to me than any other I've ever played in and I'm not going to miss it because of somebody with a sick mind. The more I think about it, the more I think it's a false threat. Please, Scott, let me play.'

Ryder pulled himself up out of the chair, a tired, worn-out man who had aged ten years in the nine months that the season had lasted. 'That's what I wanted to hear, Jackie,' he said, sounding quite emotional. 'I had to give you the chance to pull out but I'm glad you want to go ahead. We shall be taking all sorts of security precautions tomorrow. The two men from Scotland Yard will escort you to and from the dressing-room at Wembley and only the players and directors will be allowed in the dressing-room area. We are issuing special dressing-room passes and anybody not possessing one will be kept right away.'

He reached out and shook my hand, which I found quite embarrassing. It was the first time I had ever shaken hands while sitting on a bed. 'The game means a lot to all of us,' he said. 'I know you won't let us down. Have a good night's sleep and I'll see you tomorrow.'

As he closed the door quietly behind him, I crossed Scott Ryder's name off my mental short list.

On the television screen, Harvey Rhodes was wishing us all goodnight at the end of a particularly boring show.

Perspiration was pouring off him after his nerve-jarring non-interview with van der Veer. I bet if he could have got in range of me at that particular time, he would have happily shot me in my kneecaps.

14

Transcript of Tape-recording No. 7

GROVES: It's two o'clock in the morning, Ed. In just thirteen hours' time we'll be kicking off at Wembley. I'm having my usual problem trying to get some sleep so I thought I'd pass the time taping some thoughts for the book off the top of my head. I'll just ramble on and you can lift anything you think might be useful.

I had quite a day yesterday. Turner has fixed me up with two bodyguards from the special squad at Scotland Yard. They're something else. I'm not that confident about their ability to stop somebody taking a shot at me at Wembley later today but at least they're providing me with entertainment. Because my mind's been so full of the shooting threat, I've hardly given a moment's thought to the match. I'm playing this one for my dad. You know that, don't you, Ed? We've agreed to dedicate the book to him. Well I'm going to dedicate this Final to him.

The last time he played at Wembley in a Final was in the mid-50s. His total earnings including his win bonus that week was £70 and that included a fee from a newspaper for his first-person impressions of the match. It was the most he ever earned in a week throughout his football career.

My mom's still got his FA Cup winners' medal. It was dad's proudest possession. He used to spend hours telling me stories about Wembley Finals. His father was at the first ever Wembley Final in 1923 when Bolton Wanderers played West Ham. Did you know that the unofficial attendance was more than 200,000? My grandfather was one of the thousands who got in without paying. There was such a crush of people that they broke the gates down and swept on to the terraces in a great human tide.

Of course, Ed, you're a sports buff and will know all about this but I think it will be worth putting in the book for atmosphere. I'm sure there will be a lot of people who won't know the facts about that first Wembley Final. The official attendance was given at about 125,000 and more than half the £27,000 gate receipts were made up of florins. That's how much it cost to get on the terraces for that first match. It will cost £5 for a standing ticket for today's Final.

The first Final started forty minutes late because the crowd had spilled on to the pitch. A policeman on a white horse cleared them off and they sat down around the touch-lines, a lot of them with their feet sticking out on to the pitch. Bolton won two-nil and their second goal came after a spectator had stopped the ball going out of play with his foot. From that match on, all Wembley Cup Finals were organized on an all-ticket basis. Sorry to bore you with all this, Ed. I know it's all old stuff to you but just talking about it like this is putting me in the mood for the match later today.

Scott Ryder got us keyed up for the game yesterday by showing us a film of the Comets in action. They are an exciting side to watch with a lot of marvellous individual flair. But it was difficult to judge them as a team because their opposition was so poor.

The danger will come from two of their four front-runners, the Dutchman van der Veer and a flying Italian international right winger called Mario Bertolini. They link up really well together and could give our defence some headaches. Their defence is solid, with West German central defenders Klaus Hohmann and Jurgen Kress the backbone in front of that crazy but brilliant Spanish goalkeeper José Martinez. I played against him in a UEFA Cup match in Madrid a couple of seasons back. He is completely unpredictable and has been known to sit down in his goal while the ball has been at the other end of the pitch. They call him ' the ape ' because of his habit of swinging from the crossbar just to amuse the crowd. He's a great showman and also a fantastic goalkeeper. The Wembley fans are going to love him.

In midfield the Comets have one of the most skilled ball players there has ever been, the Argentinian Juan Evaristo. He's a temperamental guy but if he is in the right mood he could tear us apart with his passes. For people watching the game it should be fascinating to see Evaristo battling for command of the midfield against our Paulo Valloso. They both got sent off for fighting a couple of years ago in a Brazil-Argentina brawl in Rio, and there is no love lost between them.

The rest of the Comets are home-bred guys who we don't know too well over here but they looked as if they know what the game is all about on yesterday's film. One thing's for sure, it will be a heck of a game. There is a lot of prestige at stake for both teams. It will be odd playing against the Comets knowing that my next game will be for them but I promise that I will be giving one hundred per cent and more for United in this one.

Anyway, Ed, I don't know why I'm rattling on about the game like this. No doubt by the time you listen to this tape you will know the result and also whether my kneecaps are still intact. At least I feel drowsy now, so with luck I'll get some sleep before dawn breaks ...

. . . Morning, Ed. It's nine o'clock and I'm just off downstairs for my breakfast. I managed about five hours sleep and feel in good shape. I just called your home and got that lousy answering machine of yours. Like I said to the machine, this tape will be with the hotel porter if you want to pick it up before the match.

I don't think there's anything worthwhile on the tape for the book but it may help you in the build-up for the chapter on the Final. At least you'll be able to gauge my mood by listening to the tape.

If you want a brief summing up of exactly how I feel, I can give it to you in two words: Shit scared. It wasn't exactly the mood I expected to be in for my first ever match at Wembley after all the years I've been dreaming of playing there. But then, my dreams have never been invaded by some nut threatening to shoot me in the kneecaps. See you after the Final, Ed. I hope ...

Transcript of Tape-recording No. 7 Ends

15

WEMBLEY had never seen anything like this. A massive All-American band was jazzing its way across the sacred green turf on which Stanley Matthews had dribbled his way into FA Cup history and Geoff Hurst had hat-tricked England to the World Cup.

Dancing, mini-skirted cheer leaders were pirouetting in pretty patterns that were giving the United hooligan element something to think about beyond the boundaries of violence. Waiting in the tunnel was the band of the Grenadier Guards who would later bring the traditional sight and sound to a Wembley Final. It was a meeting of two worlds.

There were seventy-five minutes to go to the kick-off and we were out inspecting the pitch to decide which studs to wear. At the far end of the stadium, the tracksuited Comets were going through a warm-up routine in time to the beat of the twenty-four snare drummers in the band. It set their adrenalin flowing and entertained the crowd. We United players, looking like dummies out of a tailor's window in our new made-to-measure club suits, slouched around the pitch with our hands in our pockets trying to avoid the tangles of camera and microphone wires that criss-crossed the pitch in all directions.

I was sandwiched between Detective-Sergeant Coates and Detective-Constable Roberts who had not left my side since we departed the Hendon hotel at 1.15. Ken Ryan, the commercial manager who was running our perks pool, had protested when they prepared to get on the bus with me. 'No way are they going to be allowed on,' he said, blocking their entry and giving the millions of viewers watching our departure live on television an unexpected moment of drama. 'I've turned down at least a dozen requests from journalists who wanted to accompany us on the coach,' Ryan stormed. 'I don't even know these two blokes and they've not paid a penny piece into the pool.'

'They'll pay their fare at the other end,' I said, unable to take Ryan's intervention seriously. Coates and Roberts looked distinctly embarrassed.

A harassed-looking Scott Ryder came scrambling past a crush of cameramen, hotel staff and supporters crowded around the bus. 'What the hell's going on?' he demanded, wondering why the procession of players on to the bus had come to an untidy halt.

'These two blokes can't get on,' said Ryan, over-stepping his authority. 'They've made no contribution to the pool.'

I thought Ryder was going to have a heart attack. His eyes bulged and he physically pushed Ryan off the step leading into the bus. 'Who do you think you are?' he shouted. 'These two have got the full permission of the chairman to be with us. *I'll* decide who gets on and off this coach. Not you. Now keep out of my sight or I'll do something I'll regret.'

It struck me that Ryder was back to his unbalanced state and I re-entered his name on my short list of suspects.

Coates and Roberts were as jumpy as kittens in a dog pound as we walked into the goalmouth. They were suspicious of anybody that came within ten yards of me and Roberts almost got himself involved in a punch-up with a television sound engineer who had walked towards me with a small recording device in his hand. Roberts dramatically snatched it out of his hand, quickly realized his mistake and pretended he had stumbled over a wire. It was like something right out of a Laurel and Hardy film and for the first time that day I fell about laughing.

'It's all right for you to laugh, me old son,' said Coates, unable to hold back his own laughter. But then the tension of his bodyguarding job pulled him back into a serious mood. 'We're ready to fuckin' die for you today, mate,' he added with a mixture of sincerity and anxiety. 'The President of the United States couldn't ask for a better protection job. Old Taff there thought the geezer had a gun.'

I gave the giant sheepish-looking Welshman a pat on the back. 'Thanks, Taff,' I said. 'I know you were thinking of my safety but you've got to admit it was funny. That TV engineer thought you'd gone completely potty.'

The three of us broke into renewed gales of laughter, drowned out by the brassy, bouncing blare of the All-American band as it paraded behind the goal.

We walked towards the centre-circle, with Coates looking over his shoulder at the band with what was suddenly more than passing interest. He then tested me with a theory that did nothing to ease my mind as I attempted to get into the right mood for the match. 'I didn't expect to find nine million bleedin' Yanks parading around the pitch,' he said. 'Did you have any enemies in the States who might have sent that note?'

Now was not the time or place to go into details of my experience in Fairmount with the farmer. I shrugged but before I could give him any sort of answer I was confronted by an American television interviewer whose toothpaste smile and outrageously obvious toupee made him look like an escapee from the Muppets.

He put an arm around me as if greeting an old friend, although it was only the second time in my life we had met. I had given him a brief interview after Friday's training session when I realized from his inane questions that he hardly knew the difference between soccer and snakes and ladders.

'And here we have the American-born striker Jackie Groves, the player the Comets fear most of all here in old London town this afternoon,' he said, increasing the pressure on my shoulder until he was able to steer me into vision for a camera up on the television gantry.

'What's your mood, Jackie, with just over an hour to go before this great historic ball game gets under way?' he asked, blinding me with his toothy grin.

'I'll be glad to get the game started,' I said, truthfully. 'As you can feel for yourself, there's an electric atmosphere here and I think it will bring the best out of both teams.'

'Rumours persist,' he said, 'that you're gonna become a Comet player in the very near future. What d'you say to that?'

'The same as I've been saying all week,' I said, unable to hide the irritation in my voice. 'I don't want to discuss my future until I've got this game over. It's taking all my concentration and attention.'

'Fine, Jackie,' he said, as if I'd given him some sort of meaningful answer. 'Now what about the Final? What do you expect your role to be this afternoon?'

'It's my job to try to score goals,' I said. 'Any goal I can manage here today will mean more to me than any I've scored in my entire career.'

'Tell the people watching back home in America just why that is, Jackie,' said The Grin.

'Wembley is to my mind the home of football,' I said. 'It hasn't got the amenities or the facilities of, say, the Houston

Astrodome or the colour and festivities of the Rose Bowl. But Wembley has great traditions that make it a magnet for anybody interested in soccer. It's always been my dream to play here since I was a little boy growing up in America. This is where my dad played some of his greatest games for England. I hope to carry on the family tradition this afternoon.'

'That's beautiful, Jackie,' said The Grin, somehow managing to look emotional. 'Is there anybody you fear in the Comets' team?'

'Fear is too strong a word,' I said. 'There are several players that I *respect*. Martinez, Hohmann, Kress, Evaristo, Bertolini and van der Veer are all well known over here following their performances in the last World Cup. Any pro will tell you that on his day, Juan Evaristo is one of the greatest footballers in the world.'

'You are so right, Jackie,' agreed The Grin, who probably would have been hard pressed to name more than a dozen soccer players. 'But let's not forget that United have got some outstanding players. Valloso, Willson, Groves, to name but three.'

The Grin was clearly running out of things to say and looked quite relieved as he got a wind-up signal from an engineer.

'Finally, Jackie,' he said, 'what score do you predict? The experts seem evenly divided between United and the Comets.'

'It will be very tight,' I said, 'with not more than one goal in it at the end. I'm going to do my best to make sure that the goal advantage is in United's favour.'

Coates and Roberts escorted me back towards the dressing-room, leaving The Grin seemingly talking to himself but reaching an unseen audience of millions across The Atlantic. 'Now y'all stay by your sets,' he was saying, 'and after a word from our sponsor we'll be taking a closer look at this soccer ball game of the century ...'

Wembley had never heard anything like it.

Scott Ryder was pacing up and down the South dressing-room like an expectant father in a maternity hospital. He was giving birth to ideas as to how we could beat the Comets. Outside the door, Coates and Roberts stood guard, looking every inch like the coppers they are rather than the journalists they were meant to be. Ten paces away was the door leading to the north dressing-room where the Comet players were getting *their* battle orders.

'Now I don't have to remind you that the eyes of the world are on you all today,' Ryder was saying, his voice somewhere away in the distance as my mind wandered off on a trail of its own.

... I was back in Fairmount and dad, resting with his elbows on the counter in the restaurant, was talking about his greatest game at Wembley. 'It was for England against Spain,' he was saying in that rhythmic voice of his that sent me into a relaxed daze purring like a cat being stroked. 'It was a sunny Wednesday afternoon and the pitch was in marvellous nick. The sacred turf of Wembley we called it. It was like running on a velvet carpet.

'We had our best team out. Matthews and Finney on the wings, Morty, Lofthouse and me feeding off them in the middle. Our defence was perfectly balanced. Bert Williams was like a cat in goal. Staniforth and Roger Byrne were solid at full-back and the half-back line of Dickinson, Wright and Edwards was as safe as the Bank of England. Spain had Di Stefano, a genius who could almost make the ball talk. And Gento, a winger who was so fast that he used to be there and back before you knew where he was going. This was in the days when Real Madrid were just beginning to put together the team that won the European Cup for five successive years and Di Stefano and Gento were the kings of Spain.

'The action flowed back and forth like a pendulum. One minute we would be on top with Matthews dancing down the wing like Fred Astaire before putting over pinpoint passes for Morty, Lofthouse and me. Then Spain would get the upper hand, Di Stefano conjuring his way through our defence and bringing the best out of Bert Williams. Gento put Spain into the lead just before half-time, volleying the ball into the net after sprinting on to a pass by Di Stefano. Lofty headed an equalizer from a Finney cross on the hour. Then, with just five minutes to go, Matthews magicked his way past three Spanish defenders and Morty nodded his centre down in front of me. I caught the ball on the half volley and it whistled into the top of the net from just inside the penalty area. It was the greatest moment of my career ...'

'. . . the pride and prestige of United,' Ryder was saying as I returned from Fairmount to the Wembley dressing-room. All the players were going through their usual pre-match rituals but with a greater intensity than usual. Paddy O'Brien was half-way through his fifty-one catches without fear of any of us being stupid enough to interrupt his count before such a momentous match. We were quite happy to ride along on the big Irishman's superstition.

The years were lifting off Ryder's face as he got into his favourite area of tactics. 'I've been handed the Comets' team-sheet,' he said, 'and they are lining-up just as we expected. It's the same side as we saw on the film yesterday so it's as sure as eggs they'll play their usual four-two-four formation. This is going to throw a lot of responsibility on their two mid-field players, Robinson and Evaristo. Robinson is a strong, competitive player but he has nothing like the class and accuracy of Evaristo.'

'Who the bloody hell has?' said Winner Williams, who had been given the unrewarding job of trying to mark the Argentinian maestro.

Ryder ignored the interruption. 'They play everything off Evaristo,' he said. 'Robinson in particular. Every time he wins the ball, he looks to give it to the Argentinian. Now Winner's the man marking Evaristo but you can all help make his job easier by trying to stop the ball ever reaching him. Right, so we all know he's a world-class player. But he can't do anything if he hasn't got the ball. Let's try to stop him getting it.'

'I show you what a *Brazilian* can do with a ball if you get it to me,' said Valloso, his pride obviously damaged by Ryder's eulogizing of his old foe Evaristo. He added something in Portuguese, his eyes flashing with menace. I don't think he was being very complimentary about Señor Evaristo. I had never seen the sleepy-eyed Valloso looking so alert and anxious to get started. Clearly he did not need to have Scott Ryder winding him up for this match.

Theo Hall, who had passed his Friday morning fitness test, was almost visibly shaking with stage fright and I'm sure Ryder's pre-match instructions were going in one ear and straight out the other. 'A lot depends on you, Theo and Leftie,' he said, facing the two wingers in turn. 'If there are weaknesses in these Comets it's at full-back. The two American boys Quarry and Baker are willing enough triers but they are short of experience at this level of football. Take them on at every opportunity and try to turn them. This is a great pitch for wingers with plenty of width. I'm hoping the Americans won't know how to make full use of the space because many of their pitches in the States are narrow and cramped. They'll think they're in the middle of the Pacific Ocean when they get out on that pitch.'

Ryder swung round and looked at full-back partners Ronnie Dicks and Roger Hart. 'You two both know you've got your hands full,' he said. 'You most of all, Roger. Bertolini is a real sprinter. Don't give him room to get up speed. Davis is all left foot, Ronnie. Keep pushing him out to the line. He tends to hold on too long and that will give us time to mark tightly in the middle. Be cautious with your over-lapping runs until we see how the game is progressing.'

Now it was Billy Willson's turn to be pumped up. He was strangely subdued, no doubt like me turning over in his mind the fact that this would be his last match for United. 'Van der Veer likes the ball played to him on the ground, Billy,' he said, impressing me with the way he had done his homework. 'He favours his right foot for shooting so try to jockey him into keeping the ball on his left. At deadball situations, I want you to take Klein and let Monty look after van der Veer. Klein is powerful in the air and likes the ball played high to the far post.'

The dressing-room door swung open and the Swedish referee Ingmar Melberg came in past Coates and Roberts who peered anxiously in my direction to make sure I was still in one piece.

Melberg, looking as if he had walked out of a Swedish holiday poster with his white-blond hair and sparkling blue eyes, shook hands with Ryder and Hugh Blackley who had been studiously listening to the Ryder tactics talk, ready to jump in at the first opportunity which the manager was in no mood to allow.

'I look forward to a very enjoyable and friendly match played in the best of spirits,' the referee said to Ryder, but loud enough for us all to hear and note. 'There is an audience of more than 400 million people watching this match around the world and I hope we show them football that is a credit to both clubs.'

He smiled as he added in his word-perfect English: 'And to the referee.' After a glance at one of two watches that he had on each wrist, he said, 'Can you please have your players outside ready to go on to the pitch in two minutes' time. Thank you.'

The years came flooding back into Ryder's face when he saw he was not going to have time to cover all his points. Propelled by panic, he started giving out instructions in machine-gun style: 'Mickey and Jackie, push up on the Germans Hohmann and Kress . . . Jackie come back with Kress when he makes his long upfield runs and stay with him until a defender can pick him up . . . Paddy, watch out for long-range shots from Kress and curlers from Evaristo particularly at free kicks anywhere within twenty-five yards ... all you forwards, look out for Martinez coming miles off his goal-line ... saw him take a free kick in the opposition half once ... try to chip him if he strays too far ...'

We were all up on our feet now, unconsciously going through our tribal dance routine. The handshakes started, this time warmer and with more force in the grip than usual. Billy Willson collected a ball from Dusty Rhodes, which he did before every match. Nobody else was allowed to hand it to him for fear of breaking the cycle of superstition. Monty Masters removed his dentures, dropped them in a cellophane bag and handed them to Dusty before taking his place at the end of the line.

Ryder and Blackley walked down the line patting each of us on the back and wishing us luck. We all had luminous new shirts and shorts on under tracksuits that had the Anglo-American Cup emblem embroidered on the backs under our names which were in four-inch high gold letters. 'We look like a load of bloody poufs,' said Leftie Wright. Nobody argued.

Ryder then went to the head of the line and led us out into the corridor after Billy Willson had given his usual battle cry: 'Right lads, let's get out there and stuff 'em.'

The note threat had been buried without trace in my thoughts during the tense forty-five minutes in the dressing-room, but it suddenly surfaced again as Coates and Roberts fell in alongside me while we stood in the Wembley tunnel waiting for the signal to march out on to the pitch.

'Have those two taken a fancy to you?' Leftie Wright asked, much to the embarrassment and annoyance of Coates and Roberts who obviously considered they were being quite inconspicuous.

Before Leftie could continue with his ribbing, the north dressing-room door swung open and the Comets came out led by their captain Jurgen Kress. As they filed alongside us we all shook hands and wished each other 'a good game'. My mind registered the fact that Valloso pointedly turned his back rather than acknowledge the existence of Evaristo who made his team-mates laugh by pointing at the Brazilian and then to his head in the gesture that was understood the world over as meaning 'loco'.

The Grenadier Guards had just finished the final bars of 'Abide With Me' which had been sung with great gusto and feeling by the 100,000 spectators. Wembley had often been called the cathedral of football and as the hymn filled the skies above the stadium I felt, standing in the tunnel, as if I was down in the crypt of a church.

There was a signal for the teams to start the long walk to the middle of the pitch and the two queues of players suddenly started moving forward side by side as if on a conveyor belt. Coates and Roberts came as far as the end of the tunnel and then stopped their bodyguarding duty. I was on my own. Deep down, I had made a promise to myself to be perpetual motion on the pitch. Just in case a madman with a gun had got past the Wembley security guards. Or a mad woman.

As I walked away from my two minders, Coates shouted something like, 'Good luck, me old son.' But I couldn't be too sure because the noise was deafening, as the cheers of the crowd mixed with the American band playing the Battle Hymn of the Republic. A thousand red, white and blue balloons were released and suddenly there was an explosion at my feet that made me literally jump two feet in the air. Somebody had thrown a firework from the terraces. I collected my startled senses and pretended that my sudden leap was part of a warming-up exercise.

We lined up either side of a nine-foot wide red carpet which snaked off the pitch, over the surrounding greyhound track and to the foot of the stairs that led to the royal box.

We were each of us introduced to Prince Philip and the American Ambassador to London and half a dozen faceless executive officials of the Football Association, the Football

League and the North American Soccer League.

Then we had the first contest of the afternoon. The Grenadier Guards versus the All-American Band. First the Guards played the National Anthem, which was well bellowed by the United fans. Then the All-American Band belted out the Star Spangled Banner and from the volume of voices coming from the Wembley stands it was obvious the travel operators had made a fortune flying in New York supporters.

The pomp and ceremony over, I turned and did a warming-up run from the centre line to the goalmouth chipping a ball into Paddy O'Brien's hands on the way.

My adrenalin was pumping at maximum output as I felt the firm Wembley pitch giving just slightly under the tread of my studs, pulling lightly at my calf muscles. It was this pull of the springy grass that caused so many cases of cramp in the long history of Wembley Finals.

Everything was just as dad had said. Even the sun was shining. It was like running on a velvet carpet ...

16

WE were all so full of our own thoughts that none of us gauged the highly emotional and excited state into which Paulo Valloso had pumped himself. He went into the game like a time-bomb and it took him just one minute to explode. From the kick-off, Klein and van der Veer exchanged passes before pushing the ball back to Robinson who immediately squared it into the path of Evaristo.

The Argentinian was stroking the ball forward, imperiously upright and arrogant as he looked for where he could do most damage. Suddenly, with the crowd making a roar like a clap of thunder, Valloso took off at top speed as if long jumping and hit Evaristo with a thigh-high tackle.

He should have been off there and then but the Swedish referee bowed to the pressure of the occasion and weakly let the wild-eyed Brazilian off with a warning. It was one of the worst fouls I had ever seen and the wonder was Evaristo was able to play on after treatment.

As the Comets prepared to re-start the game with a free kick, I shouted to Williams: 'For Christ's sake tell Paulo to keep away from Evaristo. Otherwise they'll both be off again.'

I had Jurgen Kress standing a yard from me. We had played against each other several times when he was with Bayern Munich and captain of the West German international team. 'What is this man – a maniac?' he asked, gesturing towards Valloso who was brooding in midfield as Robinson and Davis told him in good old Yankee language what they thought of his tackle.

'He doesn't think too highly of Señor Evaristo,' I said to Kress, with a shrug. 'You need to study the history of Brazil-Argentine rivalry to understand it.'

In the third minute, the two South Americans clashed again. This time with the ball nowhere near them. Evaristo spitefully aimed a crafty kick at Valloso's ankle as he ran past and the Brazilian angrily retaliated with a wild punch that caught the Argentinian high on the temple.

Evaristo fell as if he had been struck by a punch from Larry Holmes. It was theatrical stuff but this time the referee could not duck his clear duty. He reluctantly held aloft a red card and pointed Valloso in the direction of the dressing-rooms.

Valloso reacted by kicking wildly at Evaristo while he was on the ground. The Argentinian jumped up and had to be restrained by two team-mates as he attempted to butt the player he had been sent off with for fighting the last time they had been on the same pitch. In South America, grudges are not easily forgotten.

Hugh Blackley came running on to the pitch, put an arm around the still-blazing Valloso and walked him slowly towards the dressing-rooms. His Final was over almost before it had begun. As he moved away, Blackley called over his shoulder at me: 'Jackie, the boss says you're to drop back into midfield.'

Now I really *had* to be perpetual motion. Sniper or no sniper.

With his sworn enemy off the pitch and only ten men to play against, the magnificent Evaristo began to take charge of the match. He was ghosting past the challenges of Winner Williams as if the big-hearted Welshman wasn't there and spraying out passes that were pulling our defence apart.

We all offered up prayers of thanks for the presence of Paddy O'Brien as he made three blinding saves in quick succession, two from low right-footed shots from van der Veer and one from a thudding header by Klein after Bertolini had hurtled down the right wing like an Olympic sprinter.

Then, just as it looked as if we were going to be slaughtered, we were presented with a goal from out of nowhere. The mad Martinez came too far off his line as Theo Hall fired over a speculative cross meant for the head of Mickey Dixon. Martinez had to stretch back with one hand to try to stop the ball reaching Dixon and finger-tipped it into the Comets' net.

Twenty-five minutes gone and somehow we were one-nil in the lead. Martinez ran round his goalmouth pulling at his hair in rage while we celebrated our unexpected gift.

It looked as if Martinez had lost his concentration and composure and two minutes after the goal I got the chance to put him to the test. I was in possession twenty-five yards out and fired in a rising left-foot shot that seemed bang on target for the top right-hand corner of the Comets' net.

But the unpredictable Martinez swooped across his goal like a bird in flight and plucked the ball out of the air. It was an incredible save and United players and supporters joined in the thunderous applause for this moment of sheer brilliance.

His confidence restored, Martinez regained his old bounce and humour and started bowing to the crowd who loved his showmanship. As Kress came running past me to help prompt a Comet attack he shouted: 'Yet another maniac.'

Our shock goal had knocked a lot of the rhythm and style out of the Comets and Winner Williams was managing to make Evaristo less effective by intercepting passes meant for the Argentinian.

I was covering more ground than a park keeper as I hustled and bustled in midfield but I knew that playing so deep I was not going to get the Wembley goal I had always promised myself. And my dad. I consoled myself with the thought that I was doing so much direction changing at sprint speed that only a crack marksman could have hit me with a shot and I knew there were no West Point graduates on my list of suspects.

A minute before half-time, the Comets looked certain to equalize. Bobby Davis, a stocky New Yorker who had been voted All-American Soccer Discovery of the Year, tricked his way past Ronnie Dicks and laid the ball back into the path of van der Veer. The Dutchman shifted the ball on to his right foot, shuffled past a wild challenge from Billy Willson and aimed his shot wide of the advancing Paddy O'Brien. Van der Veer was jumping in premature celebration of a goal as the ball thumped against the inside of a post and bounced back into play, with O'Brien gathering it before any Comet could react.

'Somebody up there loves us,' I shouted to Winner Williams as the referee whistled the end of a first half in which by rights we should have been at least two goals in arrears.

I was just about to make a sprint for the dressing-rooms when I was suddenly sandwiched between two familiar figures.

'You lot must 'ave been saying your prayers,' said Detective-Sergeant Coates. 'I'll tell you what, me old son, with your luck if somebody does try to shoot you they're sure to miss.'

I laughed along with Coates and Roberts as they walked me down the sloping tunnel towards the dressing-rooms. A big-busted Comet cheer leader gave me a wet-lipped kiss and a bear-hug squeeze as I side-stepped my way through the lines drawn up by the All-American band while they waited for the signal to start their half-time parade.

'Just think what she'll do for one of 'er own players,' said a clearly envious Coates. Next season, I thought, I will find out.

Paulo Valloso had packed his bag and left the ground by the time we got back to the dressing-room at half-time. 'He was screaming away in Brazilian,' said Dusty Rhodes, who was not the type to concern himself with such details as to the exact language a foreigner spoke. The way he would reckon it, an Argentinian would speak Argentinian, a Mexican would speak Mexican.

'I tried to get him to stay 'ere,' Dusty added. 'But 'e said if he did 'e would murder Evaristo when he came off the pitch. So I thought it best to let 'im go.'

It was a little anecdote I could have done without at that particular time. For some unfathomable reason, the note threat was beginning to bug me again.

Scott Ryder swept it out of my mind with his brief summary of our first-half performance. 'That was the worst display I've seen from United all season,' he fumed. 'All right, so I know that we're down to ten men but that doesn't mean we have to concede the match. Heaven knows how we're leading one–nil. We're letting them toy with us. It was embarrassing to watch the first twenty-five minutes. You treated them as if they were from some other planet. They've only come across the Atlantic, you know. Not from Mars. They've got two arms, two legs and one head just the same as all of us.'

He gave us a few moments to dwell on this harsh assessment of our first-half display and then started the pumping-up process ready for the second half. 'Now one thing I know you've all got is pride in yourselves,' he said. 'So if only to save your faces, go out there and show how you can really play in the second half. Remember, you are on show to the world today. We want to win, lads. But we want to win in style.'

Ryder turned to Theo Hall. 'Sorry, Theo, but I'm going

to have to take you off,' he said as gently as possible, but you could see relief written all over the kid's face. The ordeal had been too much for him and even though his cross had brought the freak goal he had made hardly any impact on the game.

Now Ryder was getting his fellow-Scot Frank MacLaren motivated. 'I want you to play up alongside Mickey Dixon, Frank,' he said. 'Leftie will drop back into left midfield with Winner and Jackie, so in effect we will be playing a four-three-two formation.'

His gaze switched to Winner. 'You did better controlling Evaristo in the later stages of the first half,' he said, 'simply by concentrating on stopping him getting the ball. That's the only way to play this fella. If you wait until he's got the ball, he will take us apart.'

Away in the distance we could hear the All-American band playing 'When The Saints Go Marching In'. For a brief moment I wished I was up there in the stand watching and listening, just an anonymous face in the crowd with no responsibility for what was to happen on the pitch in the second half. I had a gut feeling that there was one helluva forty-five minutes to come.

My two minders, Coates and Roberts, escorted me back to the pitch, ignoring some insulting remarks from Leftie Wright. 'Now at the end,' instructed Coates, 'me and Taff will be waiting for you down at the bottom of the steps. After you've collected your medal we'll come straight back 'ere. Don't piss about running around the pitch with the rest of 'em, 'cos then we won't have control of the situation. Now good luck, me old son, and give us a goal to cheer for gawd's sake.'

It was the fifty-fifth minute of the match and the tenth minute of the second half when the Comets equalized. Klein climbed at the far post to meet a cross from Bertolini. He knocked the ball down to the feet of van der Veer who swept it into the net from ten yards.

Down in the tunnel, the snare drummers from the All-American band started hammering out a beat and the trumpeters let rip with another impromptu chorus of 'When The Saints'.

All the running I was doing in midfield was getting me nowhere and the Wembley turf I had always dreamt of playing on was beginning to make my calf muscles feel like jelly. So far I had done nothing to make this a match worthy of dedication to my dad.

Evaristo started to grow on the game again. Winner Williams was knackered from chasing the Argentinian and Frank MacLaren had to start dropping back to help stop his flow of passes. So now our formation was a deadly negative four-four-one, with Mickey Dixon all alone in the Comets' half.

I took it upon myself to push up from midfield to my usual position just left of centre in the attack. When Dusty Rhodes came on to treat Leftie Wright for cramp, he shouted: 'The boss wants you back in midfield, Jackie!' I pretended not to hear.

In the seventieth minute I was convinced my gamble had paid off. Winner Williams lobbed a perfect pass through to me and I evaded a tackle by Hohmann, slipped the ball around Kress and shaped to shoot wide of Martinez who seemed to have been almost asleep on his goal-line. The United fans cheered in anticipation of what should have been a goal but I sliced the ball yards wide. The cheers became curses and groans.

There were just ten minutes left when man-of-the-match Evaristo scored a goal fit to place alongside the best seen at Wembley. He skipped his way past two attempted tackles on a thirty yard run from midfield, made a pretence at a pass to van der Veer and then curled a head-high shot from fifteen yards out of Paddy O'Brien's reach and into the far corner of the net. It was a marvellous goal and even the United supporters had to applaud in appreciation. Everybody that is apart from one crazy hooligan who cleared the fencing around the pitch and came running towards us waving something in his hand. Billy Willson rugby-tackled him to the ground and two uniformed policemen frog-marched him off towards the players' tunnel.

I gingerly picked up what the hooligan had been waving and handed it to the referee. It was a broken beer bottle.

He couldn't have shot me in the kneecaps with that.

The match was in its last minute when I made the sort of run through the Comets' defence I had been dreaming of since I was a kid in Fairmount playing on our make-believe Wembley pitch.

Leftie Wright fed the ball through to me. I looked to see if anybody was better placed to achieve something but the marking was tight and so I decided to go it alone.

Ronnie Robinson came rushing towards me, committing himself to a tackle when he was out of range. I side-stepped and he went sliding by cursing himself. Jimmy Quarry cautiously backed off, trying to jockey me away from the danger area. I pinged the ball through his open legs and went past him all in one movement. Then Kress confronted me and I knew that once I was past him the path to goal was open. I dummied as if to go to my right and then suddenly switched direction to the left. Kress stumbled backwards.

As I prepared to shoot, Kress desperately stuck out a leg and tripped me up. He had destroyed my dream goal. The consolation was a penalty.

Billy Willson came lumbering up into the penalty area. 'You all right to take it, Jackie?' he asked anxiously. 'Ronnie Dicks has swallowed it.'

Dicks was the usual United penalty taker but this was one penalty I would have paid to take. At Wembley.

At long last, I could keep a promise to my dad. A goal at Wembley. It was not the way I would like to have scored it. But I knew in my heart that my run had deserved a goal.

The mad Martinez was standing on his goal-line with his back to me as I placed the ball. Melberg whistled for Martinez to look at him. Finally he had to go to him and order him to turn round.

I took a five yard run-up coming from the left. All the time I was looking in the direction of the right-hand corner of the net but I knew that I would left foot it to the left. Martinez didn't know. He couldn't have done. But he took a gamble and dived to his right. He got his right hand to the ball and pushed it past the post.

I wanted Wembley to open up and swallow me as the referee blew the final whistle. Winner Williams put a comforting, sympathetic arm around me but I shrugged him off. 'Just leave me alone,' I said petulantly. Nobody, nothing in the world could have comforted me at this moment.

Martinez, the mad Martinez, was being carried around the pitch by his Comet team-mates as if he was the Anglo-American trophy. United players were slumped on the Wembley turf like wounded soldiers at the end of a battle in which they have been shell-shocked.

Dad's velvet carpet had become a minefield. And it had blown up in my face.

All I wanted to do now was get off a pitch that I was suddenly and insanely hating. They could stuff their medal. Collecting a loser's memento was not part of my dream. I stumbled in a daze past skipping, screaming cheer leaders, their tits bouncing up and down inside their T-shirts like tethered balloons in a gusty wind.

I was surrounded by ear-blasting noise as I pushed and shoved my way through lines of marching All-American bandsmen, belting out their anthems of acclaim to the Comets' victory. To the defeat of Jackie Groves.

To the end of my dream.

The End of the Beginning

He was waiting for me in the shadows of the players' tunnel as I clattered on my studs down the concrete slope that leads from the Wembley Stadium pitch to the dressing-rooms.

Behind and above me it was sheer bedlam as a hundred thousand voices cheered or jeered the Comets' parade of the Anglo-American Cup at the end of the nerve-jarring Final.

I was action-replaying the match in my mind when suddenly he came running up the slope towards me with the urgency of a man chasing a departing bus. My thoughts blurred and reeled like a film coming off its spool. It was all happening in slow motion and it seemed like hours before I realized that it was George Stoughton, holding a gun.

'Groves, you bastard!' he shouted as he pointed the gun in the direction of my kneecaps.

Je-sus, I thought, what a way this would be to end my book ...